HEART LOVE'N COWBOY

Billionaire Cowboys of Lone Star, Texas,
Book Two

HOPE
MOORE

Forever Love'n Cowboy

Copyright © 2022 Hope Moore

Heart Love'n Cowboy

She lost the love of her life; now she's looking for a new start that has nothing to do with her heart.

Looking for the love of his life, he sees quickly that she's had what he wants and isn't interested in risking her heart again. But her sweet daughter has different ideas...

In this town full of sweet, inviting people, can Sydney Ross find the new start she and her daughter need? Her grandfather gave her a hint of where she should begin again when he left his home in Lone Star, Texas, to her, but she hadn't taken the suggestion. Now, after someone from the town inquired about buying the house to turn it into a bed-and-breakfast, she's rethinking her life and checking out her grandfather's hopes for her. Is this sweet and friendly town where she and Hazel, her darling daughter, can take control of their lives, the place their hearts can recover from the loss of the man they'd loved so desperately? Was her grandfather right? Was the place their new start? One thing she knows for certain—Hazel loves her new home and seems overly interested in one particular cowboy herding cattle behind the house…Dustin Buckley.

Dustin had a tendency to get stuck on the sad things in life—especially where women were involved. He'd learned in college that it didn't matter whether his family had more money than he cared about, money he didn't talk about or take for granted—he'd learned where love was concerned, it got in the way. Since then, he's guarded his heart until now…the moment he met the new woman in town. The woman he can't stop thinking about—the woman who wants nothing to do with him.

Can the sweet and hopeful town of Lone Star, Texas, work a miracle and give Sydney and Dustin help in finding love that waits on them? Can Hazel get what she wants?

This is a heartfelt love story of overcoming loss and embracing what life offers—wonderful memories to cherish and new beginnings full of love and laughter with a heart love'n cowboy.

CHAPTER ONE

Sydney Ross sat on the back porch of her grandparents' home. The home they had left to her—well, her grandfather had left it to her. Her sweet grandmother had died several years before him, and her own loss hadn't happened until after they'd lost her grandmother. But, sadly, Grandpa understood loss very well. He'd wanted her here, and he knew before she did that she was where she needed to be.

She glanced down the sides of the three-story home that her grandparents had built—why they built such a large home, she still wasn't sure. But she did have family; she had a couple of uncles and aunts, and she did have two nieces and a nephew. But they all loved the city and that's all she could figure out as to why her granddaddy had left the house to her, and her alone. He had told her he wanted her to have a place to restart after losing her beloved Nelson. She had mourned inside—still was—but she had fought hard not to let darling Hazel be subjected to that all the time. She did a lot of crying behind doors in the three years since losing the man she loved with all of her heart. Hazel was eight; she'd been five when he died and Sydney was so glad that Hazel had been old enough to have a loving memory of her father. She'd loved him so much, just as he'd loved her.

She and Hazel both missed the family they'd been. The fun times, the adventures—trips to play out in the fields instead of hanging out in the city all the time. Nelson had also enjoyed coming here to Lone Star and spending time with her granddad. She could still remember him looking at her and saying, "You really fit in here, sweet Syd."

She blinked back tears. He'd always called her Syd, and she'd loved it. She'd never had a nickname until he'd given her that one because he'd said she was strong and feminine. *Oh, so feminine*, he'd say, cuddling her. She smiled, thinking of those moments. But she was also strong, he'd add, uplifting and had a way of making him smile that no one had ever had…

Tears filled her eyes and she tried hard to fend them off. Oh, how she missed that wonderful man. He'd been a fireman, a hero both in home life and outside life, and he'd died saving a child from a huge apartment fire. Though she hadn't been there watching, she could see him in her mind going in and saving that child. His buddies, his fire crew had told her how strong he'd been, that he'd gotten that child out through horrible fire and destruction, just as they were all called to exit. As he came down the stairs, the ceiling had caved in, and he'd tossed the child forward to Lex, his partner who was ahead of him. It was just in time for Lex to catch the child and see her sweet husband go down as he spun toward the doorway and raced to carry the child to safety.

Her wonderful, amazing husband had died in the falling, burning building but he'd saved that child.

Her heart tore open just thinking about it. Her throat clinched tight as she fought back a moan of pain. She knew in the moment he'd died he'd been thinking that if that had been his child, he would have prayed and hoped someone like him would have been able to save Hazel. She wiped her palms across her wet cheeks, fighting hard to stop more tears from flowing. She had to get rid of all this emotion before Hazel came downstairs.

Nelson had been the best man she'd ever known, and she had to do and be what he'd said she was. She had to be strong. She had to shine light and happiness so their sweet girl would have exactly that. The night of that dance here in Lone Star—the dance she'd attended to see whether this was where she was supposed to come, as her grandfather had felt she should do—had been a good evening, and all the ladies who had put it together had been fun to watch. Josie Jane and Ruby—who she knew because they'd always lived here and been friends with her grandparents—had, along with the new store owner in town, Genna, who was about the same age as her, created that fun night.

From what she'd gathered, Genna had a client of her online store who came to her physical store and asked whether the town ever held dances or things like that. The lady had a daughter she wanted to bring to this lovely little town and hopefully she could find someone to love. Sydney smiled thinking about that, because she'd heard they'd come to the dance and that now the daughter was working at Genna's store to enable the soon-to-be newlywed to have some time off to enjoy her newfound love. Sydney totally understood her reasoning and hoped it all worked out great for Genna and the new lady in town. Well, she was officially a new lady in town, too, but she wasn't looking for a romance. She had had her lifelong romance and was here for a new start for her and Hazel.

That young woman would be able to help at the store when Genna and West went on their honeymoon. And after, when Genna took time off to spend with her husband and not work all the time. It was nice thinking about how love and interest seemed to work together sometimes. Genna had an infatuation with goats, and it had just so happened that West raised goats on the huge Buckley Ranch. And the goats had played a part in their getting together. It was cute, sweet, and sitting here in the morning, it made Sydney smile. Everyone talked about how those cute, playful goats had been in the Buckley family since their grandmother and grandfather had married. The grandfather had been a cattleman and rancher, and the grandmother was from a goat-raising, farming family, and they married and combined the mix with their love.

She'd been crying and now she was smiling, it was so perfect. It was just the cutest story and she loved cute stories of romances that were meant to make a person smile. She and Nelson had had a sweet beginning to their marriage, too. Her roommate's cat had gotten out when she was taking care of it, and it had climbed high in a tree and wouldn't come down. After hours of waiting, she'd called the fire department and Nelson had come to her rescue. He'd climbed the tree and the cat had cuddled around his neck as he'd come back down to the ground; then it had sprung from him and raced into the opened back door. And she and Nelson had been left there, smiling at each other. And they'd never stopped until the fire.

She could still remember the moment their eyes locked and the jolt of electricity that flowed through her.

It was not something she'd ever experienced before and not something she ever expected to experience again...not something she was looking for. Love was a beautiful thing, and she knew it firsthand. Her love story hadn't lasted as long as she'd hoped, but still, it was straight out of a storybook. Oh how she'd yearned to live a long life with that man, but she couldn't linger on his loss. No, she had to celebrate his life, his love, and she had to smile. Because she could feel him beside her, urging her on. Urging her to put that beautiful smile he always talked about on her face and step forward with determination.

Tears surged up once more as she heard small feet snapping on the stairs—stairs she'd told Hazel not to run down. Then her sweet, vibrant daughter, so much like her daddy, raced out the back door. Hazel yelped with joy as she crossed the porch and then sprang out into the air, arms wide and legs soaring above the ground. She landed in the grass instead of the stone pathway, and she spun, grinning at her mom. Her beautiful eyes danced with joy. She loved this place, and it showed on her face and the exuberance she displayed.

"It's gonna be a great day, Mama. Yes, I know starting on Monday that I have to go to the last bit of school. But I'll get to meet kids here in town, so that's okay. It's going to be a great weekend. It's a pretty day, so you up for an adventure?"

She laughed, couldn't help it. "I don't know. We just got moved yesterday and the truck had barely left before we had to lay down and sleep. So I figured you'd be tired today."

"No, I'm not tired. I'm ready for adventure. I want to go out there—" She spun to the side and pointed out across the fence and pasture to the trees. "You see those trees across the pasture? I want to go there. When I used to stay here with Great-Grandpa, he'd take me over there to see the creek. I want to go see."

"Maybe not toda—"

"Mom, come on. I'm a big girl now so you don't have to hold my hand. Just come with me. I want to go, so please."

She couldn't help it; she stood. "Okay, but let's go in the house and get some water to take with us."

"Mom, see?" She spun so her back faced Sydney.

"I have my water backpack on. I'm ready."

Her girl wore the little water container that strapped across her back so much Sydney didn't even notice sometimes. Nelson had given it to Hazel and she loved it mostly for that reason. Plus, she could sip on water whenever she wanted to because of the way the straw was attached to the shoulder strap.

"Perfect. Then let me go get some water. Do you need to run to the restroom?"

"No, ma'am. I already went, and if I need to go, I know where the bushes are and I know how to…pee in a bush."

Sydney couldn't help but laugh. "Okay, okay. Yes, I know. When I was your age and came to visit, I would have to do that sometimes too. All right, give me a minute. Wait on me."

"Of course. I'll be by the fence."

Sydney went inside and reached into the box she hadn't unloaded and grabbed a water container. She flipped the lid open and filled it with water and a bit of ice, then she carried it in her hand and walked outside. Hazel stood by the iron rod fence, her arms on a middle rung. She had her ankles crossed at the bottom and her chin resting on her crossed arms as she stared across the pasture. Thankfully, today there were no cattle out there, but she knew the Buckleys would rotate their cattle and eventually there would be some out there. They had a lot of deer that had always moseyed around out in the pastures, nice and calm. Today, she had an energetic, heartwarming little girl to watch.

"Okey-dokey, I'm here. Let's let this adventure begin."

Her child looked up at her with those daddy eyes of hers—shimmering hazel. The radiant color was amazing.

"Let's do it!" she exclaimed. "You can go first, Mama. You can get through the fence, right?"

"Yes, dear. When I was your age, I climbed that fence many times, and I can still fit through those bars." She chuckled as she bent over, lifted a leg through and followed with the rest of her body. It felt good, actually, bringing back many memories of going on adventures.

"Hey, that was great!"

"Glad I entertained you. Now it's your turn. Here,

let me take a picture of you. Somewhere in the house, Grandma has some photos she took of me."

"Awesome. I'll have to find them." With that, Hazel scurried up the fence and sprang to the ground as Sydney snapped several photos with her camera and chuckled as she did so.

"Oh goodness, Grandma would have loved that."

Hazel laughed and then grinned. "She would have said, I was…agg—let me think, ag—*agile*. Am I right? Isn't that what she used to say about me?"

Sydney hugged her girl. "Yes, when you were a toddler, she'd say that you were one active, agile little girl."

"And you'd say, I was just like my daddy."

Sydney's heart cinched tightly and she fought off the pinching tears of remembrance. She hadn't said anything to her child about what today was, but it was the death date of her daddy and one of the reasons her emotions were plugging away at her so strongly. This was not the time to cry. "Yes, you are so much like your adventurous daddy."

She plopped the phone into her pocket and then

looked out over the pasture. "Now, as we go across here, you be careful and watch the grass. It's not too high and you do have your boots on, but we still need to watch out for what might be roaming around in the grass. You watch out for snakes and things. Watch your steps."

Hazel gave her a firm look. "I will, and you do too. Okay, here we go." She grinned and started across the pasture, and just like she'd been taught, she watched the ground as she stomped her way forward.

Sydney had a good feeling that that was how her sweet girl would approach life and the thought made her smile. She'd put one foot in front of the other and tromp along, making a path for herself that she would love.

Sydney felt her heart relax with love, and followed her girl. *Their* girl. This was going to be a wonderful day.

CHAPTER TWO

Dustin Buckley leaned forward in his saddle and used his right arm to push the tree branches up and away from him as his horse moved forward on the path along the edge of the gully. He stared down the hill that the cattle trail he was following wove down, a trail that made riding his horse on a bit easier. They'd bought this land from good ole' Johnny Foster after having leased it from him for years. He'd chosen to sell the land after losing his wife to a long illness and he'd moved to be near his family. And then, sadly, he'd also passed away.

It was a great piece of property and the cattle really enjoyed it. But they'd lost two cattle in the last month— dead cattle that hadn't been listed as sick were found eaten. By coyotes, they'd presumed, but he'd thought almost instantly that a mountain lion was the culprit. By the time they'd found the cows, they'd been pretty much devoured by coyotes and buzzards. If there had been any mountain lion paw prints, they'd been destroyed by all the coyotes that had picked over the remains. Still, he didn't think that was what took the two cows down in the first place. Coyotes always roamed the ranch and yes, if a cow was sick, there was a small possibility it would be attacked by a coyote. But usually it was only after they'd died that they set in and cleaned up. These cows had both been listed as ready to carry another calf and instead, they'd become food for what he was fairly certain was a mountain lion.

It hadn't worried him at first, not terribly; it wasn't like a mountain lion roamed the land always. Instead, they hid out during the day and came out during the night. And they didn't stay in one area long. They traveled alone and forward, not usually making a spot a permanent home. He knew all of this but hadn't thought a lot of it until now. Now that Sydney Ross and her daughter had moved into the house Johnny had left to them. He sold all the ranch land to Dustin's family but saved the beautiful home for one particular granddaughter named Sydney, who he remembered a little from when she'd visit in the summers years ago. She was a widow with a little girl and had inherited the place and had finally decided to move into it.

He'd heard this info at the diner this morning, and his attention had gone on alert. They were moving in now and his mind instantly went to the suspicion that there was or had been a mountain lion on the ravine just across the pasture from where they were going to live. He had immediately gotten up, gone home and loaded his horse into the trailer. Gotten his rifle and come out to take a look as he should have already done. He didn't want to take any chance that Sydney and her daughter would run into problems.

He'd heard from Josie Jane and Ruby that they were going out tomorrow to help them unload boxes if they needed it and to find out whether she was going to turn the place into a bed-and-breakfast. Poor girl. He hoped she had plans to open it as a B&B—not that he would do that—but he sure knew by the bright lights of hope shining in those two ladies' eyes that they were hoping she would. And, after that town dance that they'd held, he'd heard they were thinking a B&B would be great. Probably a draw for the town to have places people could stay. From what he'd seen and heard, everyone had a great time at the last party. Including his brother West.

Yes, after that dance, his brother's life had changed and they were having a wedding in a week. He was excited because this was the first of all of his brothers and his cousins to get married. His parents were walking on clouds, they were so happy. His mom was hoping they'd have a baby right off the start. West had laughed and told her not to get too excited yet, that they were living life together at first and they had plenty of little kids out there on the ranch for now. Of course, he was talking about all those baby goats. And there were a lot of them.

Their mom had been holding a dish towel and popped West with it on the hip. "I know that." She'd laughed. "But I still can't help hoping."

Dustin grinned, thinking about the play between his brother and his mother. It had been a fun moment.

Now, he was near a curve in the downhill trail, and he'd be able to start the horse walking along a trail that was midway up the ravine from the water. Suddenly, he heard a splash and laughter that interrupted his thoughts.

Where was that coming from?

He directed his horse to move forward quickly through the brush, down the ravine. As he rounded the curve, where he would be about fifteen to twenty feet above the water below, he ducked to miss a tree limb, then looked up just in time to see a beautiful sight…mother and daughter having a moment full of smiles.

Sydney, he assumed, stood on a thin spot midway up the incline across the creek, and she was laughing with her young daughter. And as he watched, the little girl reached down and picked up a rock, showed it to her mom, then threw it out over the water. It sailed through the air and then splashed into it, exactly the sound he'd heard seconds ago. They laughed; then the girl threw her arms up in triumph and Sydney, laughing hard, bent forward and squeezed her daughter in a tight hug.

It was sweet and made him smile as he watched the

happy scene. He didn't chuckle or make any noise, not wanting to interrupt the moment. Then Sydney rubbed her hand on her daughter's hair, and as her daughter's shining eyes held hers, Sydney stepped back. Suddenly, as if in slow motion, he watched as her foot slipped on the edge of the incline and she had nothing to stop her from taking flight.

Her hands went up in the air. She let out a squeal, realizing what was happening, then down the hill she went. She fell backward; she flipped in the air, then rolled down the incline. Then, upon hitting the edge of a larger ledge, she flew through the air.

Instantly, he was in motion. He spurred his horse forward and they charged down the hill through the brush. Thankfully his horse had good footing and didn't stumble. As Sydney splashed into the water, he was close enough to the water's edge that he threw himself from the saddle and into the creek.

Had the water been deep enough to protect her?

He'd jumped in, prepared for mid-depth or deep water, but she'd flown in headfirst, and he was terrified for Sydney's safety as he landed in the water. He skimmed just below the surface then resurfaced with his eyes searching the water. Thankfully she came up not far from him, having gone deeper than he had because of her angle.

But thank God she'd come up.

He could see her face from the side, and her shock was clear as she struggled to stay up, her attention up the hill as she screamed at her daughter in a surge of coughing words. "Don't come down here!"

Her daughter was screaming too, trying to figure out how to get to her mother. They were so overwhelmed by everything that neither saw him as he stroked hard across the thankfully deep water to reach her.

"I'm here. I've got you," he said as he reached her from behind and slid an arm around Sydney. She jumped instantly, then twisted so she could see his face as he looked up at her daughter. "I've got her," he called. "Stand back and I'll bring her to you."

Then he met Sydney's vibrant emerald eyes. Even with her wet hair and water streaming over her, she was beautiful, and as strained as the moment was, he was captivated.

"Where did you come from?" she gasped.

He yanked his crazy mind back to reality. "The other side of the creek. Now, relax. Take a deep breath. I've got you. We're going to move across this water to that bank right there."

"Thank you for being here." She gulped, not relaxing. "I think I'd have made it. Thank goodness this isn't a fast-flowing river."

He stared calmly at her. "Breathe," he coaxed. She didn't look away and finally she took a deep breath. His arm had slipped up and was now wrapped around her lower ribs and he felt her lungs rise as air filled them.

"There you go. I'm glad I was here, too. You're okay now but there was a chance you could have hit your head on something and landed in that water unconscious. The thought scared me to death."

"Scared me too." She looked up into his eyes. "I was frightened that she would witness something awful happening to me and I couldn't help her. Worse, it could have been her and not me. The whole situation was stupidity on my part."

"I'm going to take you to her now." He pulled his eyes from hers and leaned to the side, taking her along with him as he started to move his free arm through the water and kick his booted feet. Soon, in just a few strong kicks through the water, thick, muddy ground enveloped his boots. He almost stumbled on a larger rock but kept his balance. He kept her pulled hard against him to make sure she would be able to walk when he reached firmer ground. He felt her body become lighter as her footing found the muddy ground.

"I'm not going to let you go ye—"

"Ouch." She gasped and stumbled in the water.

Instantly his grip tightened around her, pulling her close, her back against his chest. "Are you okay?" She looked up at him, her lips not far from his, sending waves of awareness flowing through him. He almost stumbled looking at her.

"I-I just stepped on a large rock."

Focus, man. "You okay?"

"Yes, thanks to you."

The ground was firmer now, and the water was only waist deep. "I'm glad I was near." And he was. It didn't matter that his boots were ruined or that he'd probably lost his phone. What mattered was that she was safe.

She was now moving in the mud too. She was a little bit shorter than him and had to look up at him as she sucked in a shaky breath. "The fact that *I* let my sweet daughter stand that close to the edge and it was just one step back…well, again, it was stupidity on my part. I'm very grateful that you were wherever you were and saw me."

They were both breathing heavily as they progressed through the mud and water, up the incline and finally out of the water. They stopped at the edge of the stream with water dripping from them as she leaned back against him, getting a deep breath of air and obviously using him for steadfast security.

The feel of her against him, not because he was saving her but because she felt comfortable knowing he was there, had him breathing deeper than he had been.

"Mama, are you okay?"

Sydney looked up at him and blinked back tears before looking up the incline at her girl. "Yes, sweet Hazel. I'm okay." Her eyes lingered again on him and he felt the appreciation she was feeling. "Can't you see I had a cowboy hero come down and rescue me? We live among them now."

The little girl squealed, raised her hands up into the air, and jumped. "I'm so happy we're in cowboy country. Thank you, sir. Thank you so much for rescuing my mama. You coming up here? I want to give you a tight hug."

His heart pounded as he stared up at the girl. He was so glad he'd been here. "Yes, I'm coming up." He grinned at her. "But please, stop jumping and step back, or you might be rolling down the hill next. Your mom was very lucky. There's a trail just a little farther down and you two could easily get down it. If you two want to come look at the water, that's the place to do it. Believe me, cows have walked it so that it's easy to travel down, and you won't be rolling down it. I promise."

Sydney's hand on his arm tightened. "Thank you," she said softly.

"I'm glad I was here. I'm Dustin Buckley by the way." He forced himself to step back from her but continued to hold her arm. "And no more thanks needed. I'll show you the trail, and I'll know y'all are safe if you come back down here. Come on. Let's get you up that hill to your anxious daughter."

She nodded and wrapped her arms around herself, the slight breeze probably making her cold. "Dustin. I'm Sydney Ross, and that's my daughter Hazel and I can't thank you enough."

He felt it just a bit, but his mind was far from the cold, wrapped up in the warmth of her eyes. "Again, I'm glad I was here, Sydney. Now, lets get up to you daughter."

She took her first step then paused. "Are you going to have to swim back across to get to your horse?"

He chuckled. "No. When I show you this new spot for you to toss rocks, you'll see a tree has fallen across the water, and I'll walk across it to get back to my horse. I'll have to whistle for him, but he'll come running."

Sydney smiled.

Goodness, what a smile.

"Sounds like you raised a great horse."

He grinned. "I think so. I like raising them, and they

kind of like learning to do what I want them to do, so it works great for both of us." He slipped his hand beneath her elbow, and they began to walk up the hill again. "We're going to walk up this hill and I'm going to hang onto you because I don't want to take any chances. Your daughter is ready to give you a big hug, so let's do this. When we get on solid ground, we'll walk down to the trail."

"Thanks again. I would say that I could probably make it up the hill on my own, but then again it would be my luck I'd miss a step and down I'd go again."

He almost laughed but held back. "I think you'll be really careful from here on out."

She nodded, then stared up the hill and took one step upward at a time.

He followed her with his hand on her elbow for support. When they made it up the incline, Sydney bent down. This time he was there to make sure she didn't fall like the last time as Hazel engulfed her mother in a fierce hug. She clung to her very tightly, tears in her eyes as she looked up at him.

Her mother rubbed her hair. "It's okay, darling. I'm

here. I'll always be here with you."

The little girl's honey-toned eyes drilled into her mother's eyes. "Do you promise?"

His heart clinched with emotion as Sydney pulled her into her arms again. "I do, darling." Her words were rough as she tried to control the emotion he could see in her expression. "God willing."

The sweet, small girl instantly turned her head up toward him. "Thank you." And then she let go of her mom and flung her arms around his hips looking up at him as her gaze dug into his. "Thank you for saving my mama."

They'd both been through such a hard time losing her daddy and her mother's husband, and it was obvious she'd been feeling that pain again of worry for her mother. He'd heard that Sydney's husband had been a fireman who had died rescuing a little girl from a burning building. That he had managed to get the girl into another firefighter's hands as the building collapsed upon him. He'd been a hero, but Dustin felt for his family—these two sweet females.

He touched her hair. "I'm glad I was here so God

could use me. But I think your strong mother would have been fine without me. She didn't hit anything rolling down that hill, so she came up fighting to get back to you." His gaze went to Sydney, and she silently said, "Thank you." He gave a small smile and then looked back at Hazel. "You ready to see the place you'll enjoy throwing rocks at?"

"Yes." She beamed as she turned and headed up the hill. Thankfully, this part was far less steep than what Sydney had flown down.

"Can't wait," Hazel called over her shoulder as he let Sydney go ahead of him up the hill.

They reached the flat land where Hazel was waiting. "Okay, which way?"

He chuckled and pointed behind her. She immediately spun and started walking through the grass.

"Watch where you're going," Sydney called.

"You too, Mama," Hazel called over her shoulder.

"I guess I earned that," Sydney said softly, her eyes meeting his.

"You handle it well." He smiled at her and was happy to see her emerald eyes get a flicker of spark in them.

"Thank you again." She chuckled and he felt like tingles of joy were moving through him.

What was he thinking? "You've said that enough. Okay, hold up, Hazel," he called, refocusing on the kid rather than the beauty walking beside him. Both of them were soaking wet but he'd take it any day for the reward of these moments with her. "See that trail? That's what we're going to go down. The cattle travel it all the time and have for years, so it's well developed. And the area is easy to move around in and why the cattle drink here and also cross to the other side. I could cross there too but would rather keep my boots dry, so I always walk over it."

Hazel spun and laughed. "Your boots are already wet."

He and her mom laughed too. "I was just seeing if you noticed."

"I did. I don't miss much."

"She's right about that," Sydney said. "Can't get much past that cute little woman."

"And she says I get it from my daddy, but she

doesn't miss much either, so I think I got it from her and Daddy."

"Well, I have to agree that you don't miss much. So lead the way down the trail."

She grinned, then spun and headed down the trail; her mom followed her, and he followed them both. *What a day this had been. Started out bad but turned out great.*

When they reached the wide area beside the stream, the water gurgled along over large rocks as it headed downstream.

"All right, this is great!" Hazel exclaimed, her honey-toned hazel eyes sparkling as she spun to face him and her mom. "It's a perfect place. And look at all the stones!"

"Yep, I thought you'd like that. When the water rises and then lowers along here, it leaves rocks behind. Makes it's perfect for rock throwing."

"Me and my daddy used to throw them all the time when we went out on our adventures. Mama took lots of pictures, so I'll have to show them to you sometime."

She reached down and scooped up a rock that fit

into her palm. Then she smiled at him, her eyes wide. "Hey, maybe you can throw some with me. Mama tries but she's not that good. Maybe men are just better at it."

He laughed as he saw Sydney make a cute face at her daughter. "I don't know about that. You're good at it, you said, and you're a girl but will be a woman."

She looked thoughtful then laughed. "Yep, you're right. I guess Mama is just bad at it." She placed a hand on her stomach and laughed, as her mother did too.

He grinned, watching the exchange between the two. It was a fun thing to watch.

"Hey, so are you good? If you are, you can help me because I want to get as good as my daddy was."

His heart clenched tight. This little girl loved her daddy. But he knew if he'd lost his dad at her age, he'd have been very similar to her. He cherished his dad and was thankful he still had him in his life. When he was her age, he'd watched every move his dad had made with a cow or a horse. And he'd learned everything he knew about them from his dad. Except throwing rocks. He'd learned that from his oldest brother, Ryder. Ryder just had a way with stuff and had picked it up real early.

"Yep, I learned a lot from my dad but I have a feeling when it comes to rock tossing, I'm not going to be anywhere near as good as your dad was. He must have been great."

She smiled, shrugged, and looked up at her mom. "As far as I know, no one will ever be as good as my daddy but I will give you a little lee—way. Is that the right word, Mama?"

Her mother laughed a short laugh. "Yes, that's the right word. You give them a little leeway, a little space comparing them to your dad."

"Yep, that's it, then," she said. "I'll give you space if you'll teach me."

These two were really cute. Really, really cute. And they loved the man they'd lost, and it showed so very beautifully. It was touching.

And he'd better not lose sight of that fact.

CHAPTER THREE

"So, now that y'all see this pretty, easy to get to area, and that you are both okay," Dustin met Sydney's gaze, "I guess I'll cross that log and head back."

Sydney couldn't look away from her rescuer, and felt a little kick inside as his sincere eyes held hers. "We'll head back home now and start resettling in."

Hazel looked up at him. "And next time we come to toss rocks, we'll come here."

"Sounds good, but Hazel, promise me you won't try to cross that tree I'm about to walk on. It could be dangerous."

She studied the tree then up at him. "Okay, I promise I won't walk across that big tree. But it does look fun."

Sydney watched as a smile spread across Dustin's handsome face.

"I have a feeling that I can believe everything you say, so I'm going to trust you. Also, you're not going to come down here without your mom."

"I promise. I only wanted to get Mama out of the house because we just got moved in, and she was look'n kind of sad sitting out there on the porch. So I wanted to take her on a walk. I did not know she was going to roll down that hill. Good thing you were there and you're nice too."

He studied her daughter, then his gaze flickered momentarily to her, probably feeling sorry for her like so many people did. Sydney understood it and had probably given many widowed women that same sympathetic look. She'd been wishing they weren't feeling the pain of loss. But she was in that spot and had been for almost three years, and she tried to defy the painful moments. Tried to move forward as Nelson would want her to do. He'd want her to feel the strength that was inside her. The strength he'd always teased her about. *"You're the strongest woman I've ever known,*

Syd…and I love every ounce of it." She felt his words more and more lately, like chants trying to get her to…*step away*. The very thought had her frowning.

She yanked her thoughts back to now and looked at Dustin. "We'll be heading back now. Thank you."

"You're welcome. And good luck with the moving in. I heard a rumor that you had some help coming out tomorrow."

Her sweet daughter laughed. "I heard we had a lot of really nice women coming out tomorrow. Women who used to know my great-grandma and great-grandpa and me. I remember them so it'll be fun. They knew my mom too. But anyway, they are coming out tomorrow and I promise I'll help them and not come down here."

"Good. And both of you remember, if it rains hard, for several days and not always here but upstream, water will fill up down here and sometimes all the way up to the edge of where we came down from. So you certainly don't need to be down here then. Okay?"

The man was making sure to advise them well and must see how exploratory Hazel was. "Are you going to answer the nice man?" she asked when her daughter said nothing.

Hazel sighed heavily and nodded. "I promise." And then the gaze hit him again. "And when I make a promise, I mean it."

Dustin grinned. He had a way about him, and it was quite obvious that Hazel enjoyed it too. Sydney wondered if he reminded Hazel of her daddy. She pulled her mind away from that thought and looked from Hazel to him. "Thank you again. Be careful, and if you happen to fall off while we climb back up, just give us a yell."

"I promise you I won't be falling in. I've walked across that tree a lot of times."

Hazel looked at him with bright eyes. "So I'm not going to walk across it by myself like I promised. But maybe one day you'll come here and take me across it?"

"That'll depend on if your mom says I can. And if you know how to take directions."

Hazel plopped her hand on her hip. "I can take directions. My daddy taught me how to hike and how to take directions, so I'm good at it."

He smiled, his gaze softening, probably realizing just how much Hazel's daddy meant to her. Sydney's heart squeezed tight. "She's actually right. She is good at it. She wasn't the one who fell down the hill—it was me."

"Okay then, one day I'll come out and with your mom watching, we'll walk across that log and then walk back."

The smile that flashed then stuck on her sweet girl's face reached in and slammed like a hammer to her suddenly hurting heart. Her words struck again.

"Great. I'll be waiting and you will see that I learn quickly and, honestly, I can do anything. At least that's what my dad always said—*if* I learn it first."

And with that, her daughter winked at the cowboy, then turned and started up the trail. Sydney stood there, completely shocked, and when she pulled her gaze away from Hazel, she met Dustin's eyes.

"She's a great kid. I don't have any kids, never been married. Not that I need to be saying that but I guess if and when I do ever have them…well, she's really good and I'd be really proud of her. As I'm sure her daddy is."

At his words tears rolled down Sydney's cheeks.

"Yes, he would be proud of her, and I am too. Anyway." She dashed the tears from her cheeks.

His gaze held hers. He blinked, then stepped back. "Okay, I'm going now. See you later."

"Thanks again." She then turned and hurried to catch up with her daughter, who strode up the trail as though it were nothing.

By the time she caught up to her, Hazel had just stepped onto the flat land and glanced over her shoulder. This made Sydney glad she'd caught up to her, even though she was breathing hard.

"Did you get yourself some exercise? That was part of this today because you've been saying you need to get back to exercising. And you were always in a good mood when you got through walking or running."

"You're right, that was good for me." She glanced over her shoulder and saw Dustin standing on the other side of the stream as his horse came down the trail and stopped beside him. Dustin stuck his boot into the stirrup and then lifted up into the saddle, he moved with grace and experience. Then he looked across at her. She lifted her hand and he did the same; then she turned and followed her daughter toward home.

CHAPTER FOUR

"I'm telling y'all." Josie Jane Willis climbed behind the wheel of her car as her best friend Ruby Mulberry slid into the passenger's seat and then tall, lean Millie Watts slid into the back seat behind Ruby.

Millie wasn't in her early sixties like her and Ruby, but was about fifteen years younger than them. But, like her and Ruby, she wanted to go out and welcome Sydney to town and help in any way she could on getting her and her daughter moved into the large home.

Josie Jane glanced in the rearview mirror and grinned at Millie. "We'll be the official welcoming committee, and we'll be the committee that tries to talk her into opening a bed-and-breakfast in that big, perfect home for it, if she is so inclined."

Millie placed a hand on the center of the front seat of the car and leaned forward. "I have a feeling she's going to want to do that. For some reason, that night at the last dance, I spoke to her for a few minutes and she said she liked the idea and was checking it out. Now, some people might think she was just checking out the house for somewhere she and the little girl, that really cute little girl, could live. But I'm pretty sure the house becoming a bed-and-breakfast was part of the deal. You know, she's a single mom and lost her husband. How long has it been—two or three years?"

"I think that's probably what she's talking about. It's a great place to raise a little girl, so if she thinks she has the opportunity to open a business that would give her the chance to be a stay-at-home mom, I think she will. Although I understand she doesn't really need a job after her grandfather left all that oil-leasing money for the kids. Kind of like the Buckley family."

Josie Jane nodded as Millie snapped her seat belt into place. "From what I understand, he left them all doing well. I tell you, that oil has set some of our town folks up well. And yes, the Buckleys are part of all that from having owned that land for so many years that all the land rights belong to them and no one else has the rights to the oil. Sydney's granddad Johnny was the same way; they've done well and the wells keep on pumping. That's something I don't understand—a lot of oil leases stop but these around here just keep on going. And it couldn't be to any more wonderful people than Sydney and her sweet girl, and also those Buckley boys—men. I've known them all their lives and sometimes despite how grownup and good-looking they've become, I still see them being great young fellas, loving the life on the ranch. Anyway, we all know we've worked sometimes because we have to and sometimes because it's nice having an income coming in just in case something happens that way we know we have a backup plan. But, also because we love seeing people every day. My mother loved being home all day when she got older, and I was happy for her. But me…I don't think I'll ever shut my place down."

"I know what you mean," Ruby said. "Me and my sweet Red love our business, and all of you hanging out there and all the new folks just coming in on occasion."

"Same here," Millie added. "I loved my life on the rodeo circuit but after losing my husband Hank to the bull riding he loved, I couldn't make myself go back. Thankfully I found a new, happy life here hanging out with all of you."

"Yes, we were so sorry about Hank but so glad to have you join in our fun on Main Street." Josie Jane smiled in the mirror at her friend. The woman had been a champion barrel racer until that terrible night she lost her husband. Now the town loved her being here with them. "You know, Arabella is wanting to sell her bakery but she doesn't want to hole up at home, so she's probably going to get involved at church and probably spend a lot of time sitting in my shop, knitting. And of course there are a lot of ladies who like to do that already. But Arabella doesn't want to just close up her shop—she wants to sell it. She wants it to go on, and she's hoping someone will move to town and do just that. So, anyway, I'm hoping that with the dances we're starting and hopefully this soon-to-be B&B that maybe a younger woman might see potential in our town and buy it from her. Potential—that is what I'm hoping…like you said, Millie, Sydney is here to do that, too, by opening a B&B."

"Yes, me too," Ruby added. "So here we go, to give her all the encouragement she needs to do just that. But y'all do know, as far as I understand, Johnny left that to her because he felt like it would be a good place for her to find a new life after losing her husband in that fire. And a place to raise Hazel—that little girl used to love coming here and spending time with her granddaddy."

The house was just around the corner after you drove through town. It was a little winding road with a big curve and then there sat that big, beautiful house. They had come out and looked at it a few weeks ago. Ruby had been thinking that she and Red, on top of all their long hours and hard work with the diner, might want to buy it and open it as a B&B. It didn't take Ruby but one look and real serious thought about it to know that wasn't a path they could take. Josie Jane knew she didn't have time for it or the energy to keep it up. But they both thought it would do good. Weekend traffic to their little town was strong and with the new program of doing a party at least every quarter or maybe once a month, who knew what was coming. They were having fun, and this place would be great. They weren't having a party this month because they had a wedding coming up for West Buckley and Genna, the owner of the dress store in town.

And that was all because one of Genna's online customers, Audrey, had come to town to see her new store and get a picture taken with Genna. And then to get the photo uploaded to Genna's website like so many others had done since the store had opened and been a target for all of her online customers to come to town. It was kind of crazy how that sweet Genna choosing their town as her home and opening her online store as a real store with hardwood floors could bring new people to town. And then Audrey asked for a dance, and they produced it and she brought her daughter Jasmine to it. And now Jasmine worked for Genna and would enable her to take a honeymoon after her wedding as she watched over the store.

Was this going to be a new thing for the town, single woman finding love and happily-ever-afters in their small town? The whole town was now rooting for it, and a B&B would help.

Josie Jane smiled, thinking about all of the exciting possibilities. She remembered watching all the cowboys in town that night and the smiles on their faces as they asked ladies to dance. They'd seemed to have such a good time. Well, they had good times at the town events that had no outsiders invited, so new faces and romance were scarce. But this, open to all of their combined large customer base—customers and their families—had turned out to be a great idea. And the possibilities of the single people in town finding a happily-ever-after and bringing up their families in town—it was just an inspiring and motivating idea. And Josie Jane knew this because her sweet granddaughter had found love here at a dance and that alone had spurred her to really get involved.

Now, they needed a B&B that could help more people come and enjoy an entire weekend or even longer. She smiled as the pretty place came into view and she pulled into the driveway.

"This is a beautiful place," Millie said. "I've always thought so, but even with no one living in it, the beauty still shines."

"Yes, it does. It's going to be a fantastic B&B," Ruby cooed and rubbed her hands together as she shot a smile at Josie Jane and then one into the back seat at Millie. "It's just like it is meant to be. So, come on, ladies. Let's go talk to Sydney."

They all got out at the same time and three car doors slammed one after the other, like a musical tune and a drum sequence introducing the great movie that was about to start. Josie Jane smiled at the thought. *Yes, exactly. This was the beginning of a great movie…who knew, maybe a romance.* There were so many cowboys in town, it would just be perfect. She didn't say it out loud but knew it with everything flowing through her.

As they walked up the sidewalk, the front door opened and there in the entrance was the lovely Sydney. She had the shiniest black hair, cut just above her shoulders, and when she tilted her head to the side, like she did now, it draped over her shoulder just a touch. She smiled at them, such an engaging smile, and Josie Jane knew there had to be a cowboy in town meant for her. One who, when the time was right, after the heartbreak she'd suffered a few years ago of losing her first love, could be there for her when her heart was ready to love again. If it was meant to be. She'd lost her husband a few years ago and though it was hard and sad, she'd lived through it with the help of this wonderful town. And she'd never really thought of remarrying, but she'd been so blessed to have her sweet man for a very long time. This wonderful lady had only known love for six years before her husband had died. Their sweet little girl was five when he died and was now eight.

Just when she was thinking about her, Hazel stuck her head around her mother's back, grinned hugely at them and then jumped out in front of her mom.

"Hello, y'all. Come on in. Back up, Mama, and let them in." She pushed on her mother's hips, and Sydney laughed as she backed up.

"Yes, y'all, please come in. Hazel has been looking forward to seeing you all morning. Even though we were at church for just that little while, we worked since getting home but couldn't wait for all of you to get here. You're making her day."

They followed them in as Hazel chatted away about

what fun she'd had since arriving here just two days ago. Before they could ask what she'd been doing, she dove into telling them about her adventure the day before.

They'd reached the kitchen, and Josie Jane paused at the counter and looked at Hazel. "So what happened on this adventure?"

Everyone zeroed in on Hazel as she grinned at them. Then her gaze shot to her mom, who rolled her eyes and chuckled, and then the story began. Hazel waved her arms and her face lit up as if she were putting on a play. "*I* wanted to go for a walk because me and Great-Grandpa would walk across the pasture and down to the creek and watch the water and throw stones in it. So, Mama has just been sitting around too much. Y'all don't know it, but she sits around and thinks too much. And I thought it would be better after we moved here. I know she's thinking about my sweet daddy, and I think about him a lot too, but I know he would be telling me to get up and have fun. And I'm trying. But no, Mama was sitting on the back porch, looking sad, so I decided we needed to walk and have an adventure. So she said she would go with me.

"We walked across the yard and then down through the trees down to a little spot to stand on. But we were still a long way from the water. Mama picked up a rock and threw it and it landed in the water, and then I did it, too, and Mama was hugging me. And then next thing I know, she's rolling backward down the hill, then flying through the air and into the stream and went under."

Josie Jane gasped, as did Millie and Ruby, but Hazel kept on rolling with her tale.

"I started screaming and looking for a way to get down there, but then I hear this noise and I look and see this man swimming across the creek to get to her. Mama just popped up when he reached her. He grabbed her up and kept her from drowning—Mama says she wouldn't have but still, he got her. Rescued her. And he said something to her and they were talking, but I couldn't hear them. Anyway, the next thing I know, he swam over to the shallow water and brought Mama with him and they walked out of the water. Then he helped her climb the hill up to me. I couldn't move. It was like I was watching a movie. And then he held her arm as they came up to me to make sure she didn't roll down again.

"He's one of those Buckley cowboys. Then he walked us up the rest of the hill and showed us where we should go next time we want to throw rocks in the water. Him and Mama were dripping wet, and I was a little wet too after hugging Mama and then him because he saved her. Anyway, he took us to a good place and it was where he walked across a big fallen tree trunk to get back over to his horse. It looked fun. He was so good at it, like one of those Olympic fellas who walk on those skinny bars and jump in the air and land back on it. I think he could have done that he was so good."

She laughed. "I wanted to do it but before he did it, he told me not to walk across it. He was nice and said that he was going to come over one day and we'd walk across it together. I promised him I'd wait and not try it without him. I can't wait." She grinned. "I'm going to ask him if I can get on his horse too."

Josie Jane's heart pounded. "I'm so happy you're safe, Sydney. What a great adventure. Who was it?"

"Yes, tell us," Ruby said.

Millie grinned. "Do you know his name?"

Josie Jane saw how uncomfortable Sydney was

looking, and she felt bad they were doing this to her. But then she gave them a smile and Josie Jane relaxed a little.

"It was Dustin Buckley. You know, Grandpa sold the pastureland to the Buckley Ranch. He was looking for something—as a matter of fact, I don't know what he was looking for. Anyway, he was somewhere on the trail on the other side of the stream and heard me scream as I rolled down the hill, and he rode his horse around the curve, down the incline and dove in after me. I'm forever grateful to him because if he hadn't been near, Hazel would have probably raced down that steep hill that we should have never been standing on...which he pointed out to us—very nicely, though. It was an adventure and even though I'm the one who rolled down the hill and took a flying leap out into the water, I'm very grateful that he came in after me and got me back up to this sweet girl. I did not want her coming in after me. So, I owe him a lot."

Josie Jane couldn't speak. What a wonderful— well, it was a wonderful story but had its points that could have been terrible. But thank the good Lord it turned into a beautiful story. It was a sort of dangerous opening turned into a meet-cute from a romance movie opening. Her mind started to whirl. *Could it be?* She kept her mouth shut. No way was she saying anything for now. This poor woman's husband had been dead barely three years, maybe not quite three. She knew how her heart had been when she lost her dear husband. Three years was not a long time, but still, it was a very wonderful meeting.

Ruby was the first to speak. "I think it's wonderful, and Hazel said it was probably a wonderful thing to watch. Not that I'm saying you falling and almost getting hurt really badly is wonderful, but it makes the way it turned out wonderful. You made it and, well, I don't know, it could be in a movie or something."

Hazel laughed hard—bent over and slapped her knee, she was laughing so hard. "I was thinking the same thing. I love movies and I've seen things like that in them—you know, on the movie channels it's okay to watch. I see Mama watching them every once in a while and I go sit with her. They always have funny things in them like that. Y'all know what I'm talking about."

"Yes, we do," Josie Jane said, having to fight laughing because of the rampant way the little girl was rambling off her thoughts. It was adorable.

"Okay, ladies," Sydney said, taking over the conversation. "Now that we have the story of yesterday out in the open and Dustin seems like a great guy who I'm thankful didn't get hurt coming in to rescue me, let's move on. But yes, I am going to let him escort Hazel across that log because he really seemed like he knew what he was doing, and I feel like he'll take care of her. He did have good balance and it was—" She suddenly bit her lip and looked uncomfortable, as if realizing what she was saying. "Well, let's just say he did look like he was capable of walking across anything he wants to walk across. Although I would not, like you do, Hazel, picture him doing a flip on it."

Everyone laughed, and Hazel hooted with laughter, grinning at her mother. Josie Jane loved it and was so glad she was witnessing this happiness between the mother and daughter.

"So, ladies, are y'all ready to help me? Here in the kitchen is where I could use the most help. As you can see, the movers brought in the boxes and the little bit of furniture we brought is set in the rooms. I have to go through Grandpa and Grandma's things and decide what we're keeping and what we're getting rid of. That's going to be hard but will come later after we're settled in better. Today, the kitchen is priority. Lots of memories are in this kitchen. My grandma used to cook me some wonderful meals. Breakfast was her specialty. Matter of fact, I have her recipes over in one of the drawers, and I'm going to start testing them on Hazel."

"Yummy! She used to cook them when I was here, and I loved everything she made me."

Josie Jane's interest perked. "When you, well, if you open this beautiful house as a bed-and-breakfast, doing some of those recipes from your grandmother would be perfect. She was an amazing cook."

Ruby nodded and gave a grunt. "Oh, yes she was. Goodness, I remember how good her food was."

"That must have been when I was off all those years, rodeoing so much. But I guess I didn't really know her that well." Millie chuckled. "I don't want to say it, don't want to be rude, but I'm a few years younger than these gals, so I just didn't know your grandmother very well, and I really wish I had. She sounds wonderful. I can tell by your granddaddy how much he loved her. And, well, I understand—well, we all do, we've all loved the ones we married, and Ruby is the one still blessed with that sweet husband of hers."

Sydney reached out and placed a hand on Millie's arm. "Yes, I understand. It's hard to lose the one we love. Whether after only a short few years like you and me, or a long, wonderful time like Josie Jane. So you all understand it's not always easy to start over." She paused as she met her sweet daughter's gaze. "But sometimes you're reminded of the blessing you have in life, and that sweet little girl right there...well, her daddy is always telling me that I'm blessed and he's walking right beside me while I raise our loved little girl."

Hazel crossed the room and threw her arms around her mother's waist and hugged her tight.

Josie Jane's heart swelled with love for them.

"I love you, Mama, and I know Daddy is with us still. Looking down and so happy right now." She looked up at her mama and smiled, and her mother returned the smile. "And you and me are going to make him happy because we are going to enjoy ourselves and make a good life here in this wonderful town with all these nice people." She grinned at everybody.

And everyone, as Josie Jane's gaze took it all in, had tears in their eyes. Oh, what a wonderful, wonderful scene of this little child knowing that the two of them making a good life would make her daddy so happy for them.

CHAPTER FIVE

"You sure do seem distracted," West, Dustin's brother, said.

They had eaten lunch here at the old ranch house where West lived and raised the goats that their grandmother had loved. And now they were surrounded by goats: large and small, adults and babies. He had left everyone on the porch as they drank tea and coffee and talked and watched the goats play. It was a normal Sunday afternoon. He'd come out here because his mind was busy, distracted. He watched a goat balance on a plank that was nailed in the middle to a round wooden barrel, like a seesaw. Not far away stood the two donkeys the goats loved to jump on and romp around on, just as if they were the barrels nearby they climbed up and down on. But he wasn't thinking about all the entertainment the animals were giving; he was thinking about yesterday.

"Yeah, well, I am distracted but I didn't want to say anything. Didn't want to be obvious."

West put his hands in his pockets and watched the little white-and-black tiny goats that had followed him and were now playing at his knees. They wiggled and popped up and placed their front feet on his knees, then plopped back down as the other ones tried to take their place in the game. Then they chased each other.

He watched them too, then looked back at West.

"So, Dustin, what happened yesterday that's got you distracted? Even in another world. Something bad or good? In my heart of hearts, I want to say it was good but I don't want to assume something."

Dustin shrugged and gave him a slight smile. "Guess it depends on how I look at it. It was a pleasant accident, and I'm glad I was there."

"So, what happened?"

He sighed. "I went out where the two cows had been killed and eaten. And, well, I know y'all are all thinking it's just coyotes. But I don't think it's that. I think it's a cougar, a mountain lion. But that's not what this is about. I was out there and hadn't said anything to y'all before I checked my hunch out. Anyway, I was on the back side of the creek that backs up to Johnny's place. You know, his granddaughter and her little girl have moved in this weekend. That's why I went, because I didn't want them moving in and me not looking into my belief that it could be a mountain lion. I know, mountain lions don't roam around a lot during the day and they don't normally attack people, but they can. I mean, I just felt I needed to go investigate in case it's not what everyone is thinking."

"So you really think it's a mountain lion? Now that I think about it, despite only seeing coyote tracks, you're probably right. It's been so long since we saw one, that's why we didn't think about it."

"Right. But we'll talk about them later. So I was over there and about to ride my horse down that incline, dodging limbs as I made my way along the stream, looking for places a mountain lion might hole up. I suddenly hear this splash, and I hurried around a corner and saw this mom and her daughter. They were standing

across the water, about halfway down a hill on too-small of a flat spot, and were throwing stones into the water. The mom did it and they laughed, having a good time. Then the girl did it and the mom reached down and hugged her. And when she let go of her, she stepped back and the edge gave way. She toppled backward down the hill, then popped like a ball on the edge of a drop and plunged out and into the middle of the water. Of course, I was already riding the horse as close to the edge as I could get and then dove in."

He felt the fear of the moment. "By the time I got to her, she was okay. I got her over to the edge and walked her back up to her daughter. The poor little girl was upset and watching. All I could think was, what if I hadn't been there and the mother had hit her head and gone in that water unconscious. Hazel, the little girl, could have tried to get down that hill to her mother, and it could have all gotten worse. I'm very thankful I was there. She was good and glad I was there, too.

"Then, I got her up the hill to where her sweet little daughter was standing, and they hugged. It was really touching." He sighed. "Well, I can just say that I'll always be glad I was there. So, long story short, Hazel was glad I was there for her mom, too. And watching them talk and exchange their love then reminisce about the husband and father…clearly, they are still mourning him.

"I told them I'd go up the hill and show them where to go next time they wanted to throw rocks, where they'd be safe. Plus I'd need to get across the water to my horse. When she realized what I was going to do, Hazel was radiant with excitement and wanted me to take her. I told her she couldn't go on her own and that I'd come back one day and we'd do it together. Her mom was openly thankful to me for basically looking out for Hazel. But, West, I can't explain how ecstatic the little girl was at the prospect of walking over that tree."

"Wow. What do you think?"

"Well, her dad died, and you can tell that his loss still affects her mom, but in the little girl's conversation, you can tell that her having fun is what she is doing to make her dad proud of her. I haven't been able to stop thinking about it. I saw them briefly at church this morning but I got there late and they had a whole gathering around them. I did lift my hand and waved when she looked across the lawn at me."

"Did you smile at her? And are we talking about the mom or the little girl?"

"The mom, and yeah, I smiled at her. But, you know, I didn't want to overdo it or anything. The poor woman has been through a lot."

"You're interested in her."

Dustin sighed. "Yeah, and I shouldn't be. She's not ready to be interested in anyone, and well, I just met her and I'm glad I was there. Look, forget I said all of that. I'm out here, struggling a little bit but I'll get over it. Truth is, I've watched you and Genna fall in love, and I enjoyed it. Y'all kind of woke me up to the fact that it would be good to find a mate. A wife to love one day. Someone to enjoy life with, like you two are doing now and are going to for the rest of your lives." He sighed and watched the goats having a good time.

"It's going to work out," West said.

"It's just, that right after I'm thinking maybe starting to look for love, I have this interaction with a woman who isn't looking for it and I'm drawn to her. I mean, West, you and me both know we get attracted to girls, but I've never been drawn to anyone like I am to this beautiful woman with a radiant heart. I mean, you should have seen the way she looked at her little girl."

He sighed. He couldn't say any more. Talking about it just made it all cut into him deeper. He felt really bad about feeling this way. The woman had obviously loved her husband, and he wasn't going to do anything that seemed like he was trying to intrude on her emotions like that. "I have to stay away. I've got to shut these first meeting feelings down. Don't tell anybody else what I just told you. I don't want anyone thinking that I'm going after this poor lady who's obviously lost the love of her life. It sounds terrible to me, and I don't want to be known as one of those guys."

West placed his palm on Dustin's shoulder and squeezed. "Listen, you aren't one to just jump into anything. And as far as I've ever seen since college, you're very cautious about dating women. So, for you to stand here and tell me this, and for me to look you in the face and see the emotions in your expression and your eyes…I can see it's rough. All I can say is come on, brother, be yourself. Don't hole up and ignore her. That would be rude. You met her little girl, and she is obviously very grateful to you for saving her mom. If you start avoiding them, you might hurt somebody's feelings. And as far as I can tell, the last person's feelings you'd want to hurt is a little girl who lost her daddy.

"So, just don't go making advances or anything like that. You're strong enough to be you, and you are strong enough not to come on to that woman. Just be a friend. They are moving into that house, and we're going to be herding cattle out there—you're going to be around. Plus, if you think there is a wild cat out there, then we need to make sure it's gone for their safety. So, if you need me, I'll be going out there with you. Matter of fact, we all need to be out there looking for it."

"Yeah, you're right."

"Yep. The last thing we'd want is for Hazel to go wandering off out there and something happen to her."

Dustin took in every word his brother had said. He was strong when it came to internal emotions. He'd had a really bad experience in college with the gal he'd thought he loved. But she'd just tossed him to the side. And he also knew that was something similar to what West's soon-to-be wife Genna had been through. He thought about that for a minute. Sometimes being tossed to the side helped you find the right footing and the right place. And he was so thankful that Genna had decided to take her life into her hands, and she'd moved to this town and made his brother the happiest man in the world. Next week, she was going to become Mrs. West Buckley.

He grinned at his brother. "You know, you are pretty smart. And yeah, I'm strong, and I can be there and make sure that they are safe without getting personal. So, yeah, maybe tomorrow we'll go out and hunt for the cat. Evening might be best since they might be moving around more. I'll check that out. So, thanks. I'm going to head home. I've got some things to do."

"You mean like figuring out how to catch a mountain lion?"

He chuckled. "Man, you can read my mind. Yeah, that's exactly what I'm talking about."

"Okay, so we'll see you in the morning, and we'll tell the others. There will be a whole herd of us out there, and if there is a mountain lion on our property we'll get him."

"Sounds like a plan." He headed toward the house, told them all he was leaving and that he had some things to get done in his home office. They all lived on the ranch in various cabins. His mom and dad lived in the main house. Which was, these days, empty most of the time because they handed the ranch over to him and his brothers and cousins while they were enjoying traveling. But all of them had marked a favorite spot on the ranch that they'd like to build a house on one day, a house with their family. But for now, it was cabins—all, that is, except West, who'd always loved the goats and asked to live here among them. It was a perfect choice and had made his grandparents happy knowing the goats would continue and be well cared for. Funny thing was the goats had helped attract Genna to him, so it had been meant to be.

Dustin wondered whether there would ever be a woman meant for him.

After telling everyone goodbye, he'd gone home and spent the evening researching wild cats in Texas. And he also told himself to be himself and to not let his heart get any more involved than it was.

He'd just met the woman. He could not be in love with a woman he'd just met and had had a very brief— well, a bit longer than brief—conversation with. So for him to even think that was ridiculous.

Tomorrow was a new day. And he would have his head on straight.

However, when he went to bed that night, thoughts of her and how he'd felt after helping her up that hill and talking with her and watching her with her child and the love that gleamed in her eyes filled his night with wishes that some of that would be shined on him.

CHAPTER SIX

It was Monday morning, and Sydney hadn't slept well. Her thoughts had gone to falling down the hill, being rescued, and her sweet daughter's reaction to the man who'd rescued her. And the joy she felt knowing she was here for Hazel and hadn't been hurt. She owed Dustin a big thank-you. She just didn't know what; she'd have to figure that out. *Maybe make him a cake?* She wouldn't be inviting him to dinner or anything because she didn't want to give anyone the wrong idea. Especially her sweet little daughter. But she did owe him something. She kept thinking about if she'd hit her head on something before landing in that water. What a horrifying time it would have been for Hazel.

If she really thought about it, he had been placed in the right place at the right time, and he'd been up for the challenge. She was very thankful for that. But today, there were other things on her mind. So many things that sleep was almost nonexistent. So, after she'd driven Hazel to the small school in town, she'd come to the Mulberry Diner and gotten a cup of coffee and sat by the window. She'd enjoyed seeing Ruby and her husband Red, who had come out smiling to welcome her back to town. The excellent cook was a great fella, and it was evident by the way he slung his arm around his wife's waist and hugged her to him that he cared for her. When Sydney told him she'd always loved his food, he'd grinned and told her the place wouldn't be what it was without his amazing wife. Then he'd kissed Ruby on the cheek and headed back to the kitchen. Sydney liked the way he was with Ruby, and it was obvious Ruby felt the same for him.

It had been the same for her and Nelson. She sighed and took a sip of coffee to wash away the emotional wave that almost came over her. She had to move forward.

She had to think of him without always going to tears. She had to, and so she focused on why she was here, waiting for Genna to show up at work. She focused on her new endeavor. It was the beautiful large home that her granddaddy left her and she needed to decide whether it was going to be more than just a home for her and Hazel. *Was she going to open it up as a bed-and-breakfast?* Was she going to do that and make not just Ruby happy but her friend Josie Jane? And also Genna, who she knew wanted her to do it.

Sleep hadn't come quickly. One side of her brain was saying *yes, yes, yes, do it*. And the other side was saying *no, no, no, don't do it*. She didn't have to, but did she need to?

Was that what she needed? One thing she knew was that it wasn't something Hazel would hate. No, she would love it. Absolutely love the idea of having the house full on the weekends. She'd have to talk to her about minding her own business and not bugging people to death. And, of course, the normal talk of be careful and don't go anywhere with anyone unless Mama gave the okay. It was what they'd always done in the city. Despite this being a wonderful place, it was still a rule, especially if they would be hosting strangers in their home. But she would be watchful because she'd already lost the man she loved, and she wasn't taking any chances on losing Hazel. And that was the reason she felt comfortable here.

As she took another sip of coffee, she saw Genna drive up and get out of her car. Her wavy dark hair with hints of auburn shone in the morning sunlight. She placed her money on the table, got up, and waved at Ruby, then headed out the door.

"Hey, Genna. Good morning."

Genna was unlocking the store's front door. "Hi. How are you?"

"I'm great. I have something to talk to you about."

Genna grinned and pulled the door open. "Well, come on in. I'm excited to hear what you need to talk to me about. I have my hopes, you know."

She smiled, just from the energy she got from this cool woman. She wrote the funniest articles that her online store customers enjoyed. From what she'd come to know after looking at her online retail store, Genna had moved here a little over a year ago and fell in love with the town. And her online customers were now coming here to Lone Star to visit her real store. But recently she'd begun posting about gatherings the town was going to start hosting. And that was what got Sydney's attention about it all when Ruby called about her grandpa's house and her mother told her it wasn't for sale; it belonged to Sydney. That was when she'd decided to come and see what was going on. Soon she decided to move here because her grandpa had been thinking about her and Hazel's future. Now she knew he was right. This was where they needed to be.

And the town needed a bed-and-breakfast.

She hadn't been sure about whether she would do that. But the house had six rather large bedrooms upstairs. And downstairs, there was a big master bedroom that had an attached room that her grandmother had used for a sewing room. It was a nice size and would make Hazel a good room. It was as if her grandparents had built the house with a B&B in mind. It was the strangest thing. But then again, they had hoped to have big family gatherings. They'd had some, but overall, she was the one who'd come the most in the summers. Even when her mother couldn't come, she let

Sydney and then she'd come and pick her up. While she was here visiting, she'd get to eat at Mulberry's and loved it. She lived for every moment she got to come and visit. And obviously her granddad had noticed and left it to her for that reason.

Now, as she crossed through the lovely clothing store, following Genna to the counter, she saw that all types of clothing were here: Bright clothes, casual, dressy. Clothing for younger women and older women. It was really nice. She paused at a beautiful soft peach-toned summer dress. It was really lovely. Then she walked forward and left it behind. She hadn't dressed up for a date since losing Nelson. She hadn't even gone to a store and looked at something like that, she wasn't going on any dates.

"So okay, I'm just going to turn my computer on and get it going. Customers won't come in till nine or when they get to town from wherever they're driving in from. You got here early, I'm assuming, because you dropped that adorable daughter of yours off for her first day of school here."

"You are very good at reading people's minds. Yes,

that's exactly why I was already here. I took a moment to go inside and visit with Ruby and her husband. He's really nice and a wonderful cook, so it was good to see him, too. The man is so talented, and she has a way with people. They make a great couple."

"Yes, they do. And good taste runs through him. I hope that's the way it is with me. I think I pick good clothes out."

She laughed. "I don't know if you mean that as a joke or just trying to get me to compliment you, but yes, it flows right through you. You're good at picking out clothes."

Genna laughed. "I was just teasing. It doesn't matter if I have good taste or not. People love what I buy and that right there is all that matters. So I'm not going to say I have bad taste and people like my stuff. I'm going to leave it at I have good taste and people like my good taste. I'll just compliment myself."

They both laughed at that.

Sydney loved it. She really liked Genna. She'd seen in the writeups that she did on her online store that she had a sense of humor and that she loved goats. She'd been placing photos of goats on her site because she thought they were so cute. And since her soon-to-be husband raised goats on the big ranch, living in the original home of his grandfather and grandmother, who loved them too, it was as if they were carrying on things that mattered. That stuck in her mind and it hit her then.

She loved her grandpa and grandma's home and had wonderful memories there, and the very thought of carrying on those memories with her daughter and others was what she wanted to do. The memories weren't just of her living at the house with them but of their trips to town, and laughter when they sat in the diner and laughed with Ruby and Red. That had been a long time ago but they stuck with her. And when Josie Jane would come over and laugh with them. None of them seemed to have aged after all these years, but then she'd been a kid. No matter what, they all looked great.

Suddenly, she had no hesitation in what she was about to say. "I'm going to open my place as a bed-and-breakfast. So do you like that idea?" She knew she was asking a question that would be answered with a yes.

But instead, it was answered with a squeal, and

Genna threw her arms around her and squeezed her tightly.

"You have just made me so happy," she said against her ear, then pulled back, grinning. "Oh my goodness, you've made everyone happy. Just wait till Josie Jane and Ruby hear this. And then all the others. Everyone is going to be so excited. And I can tell, you know, you're going to have business out the wazoo."

They both laughed at that, then started talking about how she would set it up. She had to get some painting done; if she could find someone to come in and do the work, it wouldn't take long. As far as she could tell, her grandpa had taken really good care of everything. He'd loved to collect things and so had her grandmother, so she wasn't getting rid of the beautiful things. Yes, she would probably get some more updated items like bed coverings, pillows, curtains, and rugs. She'd attempt to make it as plush as possible with sweet, small-town appeal. She'd mix their taste with some more modern things too. Homey and warm and romantic—she'd have to keep that in mind. Everything was running through her mind at a high speed, and she had to figure out which ones would be the romantic rooms.

The door opened and Jasmine, Genna's newly hired help, walked in. "Good morning. Sorry I'm a little bit late. There was a tree across the road on the way in from Marble Falls, so I had to wait while they got it up. Hi, you're the one who owns the large, pretty house outside of town, right?"

"Yes, I'm Sydney Ross. I know your first name is Jasmine. It's nice to meet you."

"Nice to meet you, and my last name is Scott. So, from what I've heard since I started work here last week, you're the one who might make everyone in town's day if you open that beautiful huge place as a B&B." She cringed. "I hope I didn't say something I wasn't supposed to. I mean, maybe you aren't planning to do that. I'd hate to say that and be presuming when I shouldn't—"

"Yes, it's going to be a B&B," Sydney interrupted her and smiled. "That is what I came in to tell Genna and now you."

Jasmine hoisted her arms into the air, grinning with excitement as her purse slid down her hiked arm and slammed against her chest. "Yes! You have just made my mom's day. She cannot wait for a B&B to open. She can't wait to load all her friends up from the Dallas area and come have a fun weekend. She loves this place and couldn't wait to get me here." She chuckled. "And she was right. I loved it too, and fulfilled her dream and decided to move here the moment Genna offered me the job. And I'm about to call it home and not drive in every day as soon as my boss gets married and I can move into that cool cabin she's living in right now."

Genna smiled. "West offered her another one but she likes mine and so she'll be driving in for another week or two, depending on how long it takes her to move in."

"Not long, I can tell you. I don't have that many things, and Mom and Dad have my stuff already on a trailer and ready to bring in the day after the wedding. Just like you told me I could do." She frowned. "Mom thinks I'm going to find a good cowboy since I'm moving here, but I'm just here to start over. And anyway, even though I'm going to have that cute little two-bedroom cabin, my mom wants to load all her friends up and spend time at a B&B. And yours is going to be perfect. She loves B&Bs and, well, I don't want to sound rude but my mom has a big mouth and loves to tell people about places she loves, like Lone Star. And I'm pretty sure your place is going to top the list."

Sydney's heart pounded, seeing Genna's and Jasmine's happy faces thrilled her. "Y'all's enthusiasm fills me with joy. I haven't felt this excited in such a long time. I just know it's right. My daughter is so very delighted about being here, and when I tell her after school today, she's going to be walking on air.

"We met one of our neighbors yesterday. One of the Buckley men, your soon-to-be brother-in-law. He actually rescued me out of the water. Hazel and I had gone down halfway to the water and were throwing rocks into it from a little ledge, and, crazy me, I turned to give her an excited hug and my foot slipped. Thankfully he was on the other side, and came around a corner and saw me tumble down the hill, fly into the air and land in the middle of the stream. When I came up, he was there in the water to rescue me. Even though I can swim, you never know...I could have hit my head

78

and gone into the water unconscious and drowned, and my poor baby would have been able to do nothing."

"Oh my gosh! That must be why that sweet Dustin was preoccupied yesterday at the family lunch at my soon-to-be house. He ate quietly then went out alone with the goats, and my West went out and talked to him. He neglected to tell me about how you ended up in the water. Maybe Dustin didn't tell him that part. I'll have to ask him."

"I'm glad he was there," Jasmine said, patting her arm.

Both ladies hugged her, and Sydney hugged them back, feeling the support like a gift. It was so needed.

"I am forever grateful to him. And he was so sweet to my daughter. He talked to her and made sure we got up the hill, then showed us the place to go next time we go out there. Where the cattle trail goes down to the water."

"He is a wonderful man." Genna's eyes suddenly locked on Sydney. "He's going to make someone a fantastic husban—"

"But not me," Sydney said. "I need to make that

clear, because what I'm hearing in your words and seeing in your expression are some of the same things I heard from Josie Jane and the other ladies yesterday when they came out to help me unpack my kitchen. He was great, he was…but I am not looking for what I keep hearing in the excited voices of everyone." Her voice was firm, and she knew her face was too as she looked at them. Surely these people would get the outspoken hint that she was not interested in finding love or even dating. She had loved Nelson deeply and nothing, *nothing* could replace that.

"Okay, don't get upset," Genna said. "We understand. I didn't mean what it sounded like. But I am thankful that he was there. I didn't mean to insinuate that romance was in the air. And if Josie Jane, Ruby, and Millie did, I'm sorry. I can tell you they aren't doing it to be mean or cause you pain. They just have hope for the town and all who live here. If you want me to, I'll make a statement to them that they'll get. They'll lay off, if they pressured you in some way."

"I understand," Jasmine added. "What I went through is not nice and I needed a new beginning. My mom got me here but I'm not on the market either. But I know I need to start over, so I'm here for that. Who knows—somewhere down the line, I might be open to a romance. But not now. So I fully, in many ways, understand you putting roadblocks up for everyone to be aware of. I'm jealous, actually. You knew love like I once dreamed about but have no room for right now. Right now, I'm just excited about getting a new life started here with this wonderful Genna and you. I'm so glad I came in and got to hear all of your news. And again, my mom is going to be so thrilled. So you just know that and move forward at your pace. I'm not going to encourage anyone to try to set you up in romance— you were blessed to have a beautiful one already."

"I don't know who you heard it from but yes, I did. I just don't know how I could ever find two wonderful men in one life. My heart's not into that, but my heart *is* open to this town, and I'm so excited about getting it up and running. I wasn't certain but the minute I came into the shop earlier, it just slammed into me that this was what my grandpa knew. He knew where I belonged and where my baby girl needed to be. And I'm forever thankful to him for this. So, ladies, let's let this adventure begin. We're going to help this little town and have fun doing it. Genna, you're already helping and doing a great job. And now that you have this nice lady here to help, are you going to take a little time off after you get married?"

Genna smiled. "Yes, I am. Oh, I'll be here but not all the time. I've got a yard full of kids to play with and a soon-to-be hunk of a husband to start living my dream with. So, Jasmine came along at the perfect time. And so did you."

They all grinned at one another and then, just as if they read one another's minds, all three of them reached forward and shared a group hug.

Sydney knew without doubt that she was where she needed to be.

CHAPTER SEVEN

Dustin and all of his brothers—Ryder, Caleb, West, and Zack—along with his cousins, Hunter and Ace, loaded up the trailer with their horses Monday morning, then drove to the land they'd bought from Sydney's grandfather Johnny. Once his family heard what he thought had killed the cows, they hadn't hesitated to join in the hunt. They all agreed they needed to find, catch, and move the mountain lion. Or kill it, if it came down to that.

It was unusual for a mountain lion to take down a cow but if it was killing their cattle, then they were getting rid of it—if it was still around. Mountain lions customarily moved along quickly, only in an area for a short time. Hopefully, if this was one, it had already moved on because they'd found the two cows three and four weeks ago, in two different weeks. But, even though it was across the pasture and across the ravine from the house, and long enough that hopefully it moved on, there was now a mother and daughter living there. And they all agreed that fact meant the mountain lion needed to be dealt with now if they could find it. Or maybe if it knew they were there, it would leave if it hadn't already.

Safety was key and they took it as their responsibility to look out for Johnny's granddaughter.

"I feel bad that I didn't think about this," Ryder said. "It's not normal for coyotes to kill cattle, but there were no other impressions to see and get any idea about. If we'd have found those cows earlier, we'd have known what it was because the prints would have been there. And I should have never assumed a coyote killed it in the first place. I feel totally stupid."

That was a highly unusual statement for his oldest brother to say and it told Dustin that Ryder really meant what he said. Yes, they probably should have suspected it right at first, and he was glad that he'd at least gotten the thought.

"Hey, don't be so rough on yourself. We're all a team. I got the gut feeling that it wasn't right and should have said something right away. But at least now we're all in agreement and going to take care of it. And after we search, I feel like it's my responsibility to go over and tell Sydney, for her and her daughter's sake, what we suspect."

Ryder nodded, his gaze serious. "Yeah, we can't let her live there, maybe wandering around, and not be aware of this. If something happened, we'd never forgive ourselves."

All their brothers had mounted up and all said different forms of agreement. They all wore serious expressions—the hunting was about to begin. Hopefully they'd find the animal quickly and be able to take it away. He was thankful that mountain lions were loners so there was most likely only the one—*been* one was his hope.

"Okay then, let's split up and take different areas of the place, focusing on the ravine area that runs from the connecting property through most of this property. Remember, they don't like to hole up in caves like a lot of people think. They like to sleep under cliff crevices, overhanging ledges, and sometimes badger holes. Which, as we know, this gulch area has plenty of all of that, so check them out.

"I have to tell you that I believe Johnny wanted Sydney and Hazel to start a new life here, and we need to make sure they do. This animal isn't going to mess that up. They are really nice and that little girl is the sweetest thing…but also not afraid to explore, as far as I can tell. So that worries me." His brothers all agreed. "I think her and her daddy used to throw rocks together down here, so it means a lot to her. And that ravine close to the house is some of the deepest areas, so that's where I'll be."

"Good," Ace said. "The house has been vacant and who knows what that cougar is calling home."

"Exactly," Dustin said. "If he's still around, I have a feeling this thicker area would be his spot. If I'm right and he's still holing up somewhere along there, hopefully we'll disturb him and run him out where we can catch him, kill him, or move him on."

"Let's do this," Caleb said. "It may take more than

a day but we need to get it started."

"Great. Let's get to it. But," Ace said, "me and Hunter are going to start at the lowest end of the ravine before it goes flat, and we're going to work our way in. If anyone disturbs it and puts it on the move, we all need to know so we can be ready. Just remember we're all out here, so shots down only, or things could get bad. You all know your rifle safety, so don't forget it."

"Ace," Hunter said to his twin. "You fish out here a lot, but you haven't seen anything before?"

"Not that made me think of a mountain lion." Ace's brows dipped and his blue eyes deepened with a green tone, almost as if his thoughts had darkened. "I've seen the paw prints of many wild animals, even bobcats, but they're too small to be dangerous to a cow or a person. Lots of coyote tracks are a normal thing as you all know, but they keep their distance, too. Believe me, if I'd seen a paw print big enough to be a mountain lion, I'd have said something to y'all, and we'd have been doing what we are doing now already."

Dustin gave his cousin a thumbs-up. Ace might be younger than everyone, including his twin brother, who was a few minutes older than him, but he had a good brain. He loved the outdoors, even more than just riding a horse and herding cattle. The dude *loved* to fish—as in, he probably could have gone into the world of fishing tournaments and competition, given up his stirrups for fishing rods and reels. He spent any extra time he had on the rivers and creeks of their land, and was most often alone. Dustin was glad Hunter had asked him this question because Ace was the one closest to the banks of the water on the ranch.

"Okay, good to know. Maybe he's gone and that would be best," Dustin said. "So, let's get after it. The day is going to fly, and we have a lot to search."

Everyone agreed and they headed out, splitting up into three groups. The search began with Hunter and Ace on the outskirts on the left, Ryder and Zack on the other end, and him, West, and Caleb spread out in the center.

The stream was at the bottom of the ravine and had different levels of depth and width as it made its way through the pastureland. Toward the ends, the ground leveled out and it became just a normal stream running through the land, with no hills rising up around it. It was good for cattle country. On the part where Hunter and Ace were headed, there were no ledges or washouts for a mountain lion to hide beneath, but they were going to start there where the ravine ended and work their way into it. At the other end, it was already a ravine as it entered their land but smaller, the land on the other property having flattened out like the opposite end of theirs. It was the middle where Dustin had chosen to start that was the widest and deepest and, as far as he could figure, had the most areas for a mountain lion to rest during the day before it took its excursions during the night. And that was the area closest to Sydney's home. That was near where they'd lost the two cows.

And that was where he was going to make certain the cat wasn't living. Sydney and Hazel were calling their place home now, and he was going to make sure a mountain lion wasn't doing the same.

CHAPTER EIGHT

They had searched all day for the mountain lion, hadn't even taken lunch. But at four-thirty, they loaded up their horses and Ryder drove them back to the ranch. Dustin climbed into his own truck that he'd brought because he was heading around to Sydney's place. They'd found nothing—no paw prints, nothing. And though it was a slight relief that maybe the mountain lion had moved on, he still needed to tell Sydney. And he would keep up the search longer, until he was positive the danger was gone.

But right now, he had another job: knocking on the front door of Sydney's home and telling her what was going on. He drove up the lane. It was a beautiful place, had always been, and he'd heard the ladies in town talking about what a great bed-and-breakfast it would make. And he had to agree with them. It was set up perfect for it, and Johnny hadn't sold everything. The house had a nice few acres around it, and she could use it in some way. Maybe build a pavilion out there that would be great-looking and could hold weddings or parties or reunions. There was a lot that could be done here.

The only reason he thought about all of that was because West and Genna had wished for something like that for their wedding. The church was too small because they were inviting everyone, so they were having it at the ranch. They were getting married in a newly cleaned-out barn. Not the barn at the old house the soon-to-be newlyweds would call home, because there were too many goats roaming around. They were getting married at the main ranch and his mom and dad had helped oversee the cleaning out and decorating of one of the main barns. It was really going to be fun, and knowing his mom and Genna, he figured it would be beautiful.

And everyone was excited about it.

But he didn't know whether she was opening this

place as a B&B. She and her daughter had to settle into a new life here and maybe didn't need the house full of people they didn't know. He wasn't taking anything for granted and wasn't asking questions. He was here to tell her she might have something to be worried about or at least be conscious of, so she could be sure her daughter understood that roaming around alone right now was not a good idea. Not with the threat of a mountain lion sharing their backyard of sorts. They needed to know that maybe neither one of them needed to go out there, even together.

He'd told Hazel that he would take her to cross the tree trunk and if they still wanted to, then maybe he needed to make himself available to take them. But that just sounded kind of crazy. It was like stepping on their ground. All of this would be up to Sydney. He was just here to warn her.

Yeah, he knew he could also say they couldn't trespass on the Buckley property but he couldn't do that. This used to be their property. So, he just needed to make her understand what could be at stake if that animal was still around. If it would kill two cows, who knew what it would do. He wasn't taking any chances. He knew out in California, there were a lot more people attacked by mountain lions on hiking trails or jogging or bicycling than around here in Texas. And that made him aware that it could happen.

But he was going to make sure it wouldn't be here, and hopefully she'd support his opinion. He walked up the path and knocked on the door. Almost instantly, the door flew open. He looked down and there stood a smiling Hazel.

"You came. Mama," she called over her shoulder. "He came to take us across the water on the log."

Holy moly. That wasn't what he was there for, but he had told her he would do that. He looked down the hall, then back at Hazel. "Maybe, but not today. I'm here to talk to your mama."

"Okay, but you said we would. But I guess you can just talk to my mama but maybe you can set a date with her about when we can do it?" She grinned up at him, the cute little coaxer.

He chuckled. This little kid had a way about her. "Yeah, I'll add that to my conversation with her." He looked up, hearing footsteps along the hallway. The long, wide hallway looked like it led to the kitchen. But it also had a staircase that came down from the upstairs and started here in the hall. It gave the area plenty of room, almost as if it had been built to be a bed-and-breakfast. Pretty wild but maybe Johnny had that in mind when he built it, for sometime down the road. Maybe he'd known one of his kids might want to do something like that. The man had been smart, and his granddaughter, as she came around the corner at the end of the hall looked stunning.

"Hi," she said. "So did I hear you say you need to talk to me?"

He whipped his hat from his head and held it between his hands. "Yes, I do." He glanced at Hazel, then back at her. "In private, if possible." He looked back at Hazel, whose eyebrows were now scrunched together as she studied him. "If that's okay with you. I'm sorry but I need to talk to just your mom."

She popped a hand to her hip. "I know, I know. Adults have to have conversations sometimes. So Mama, I'm going to go play. But don't forget you're going to talk about me getting to walk across that tree."

He smiled and met Sydney's gaze as she moved down the hall and now stood beside her daughter. He could tell by her eyes that she had determined something was up. She was a smart woman.

"Darling, you go play, and I'll bring you a plate of cookies when they're done. They are almost ready to come out of the oven."

"Sounds good to me. And maybe he might want some of your cookies too." She grinned at him, then raced down the hall, past where he'd first seen Sydney, and then hung a right and disappeared through a doorway.

He pulled his gaze away from that and refocused on Sydney. "I hope it's not a problem but I'd rather her not hear what I have to talk to you about from the kitchen. I assume that's where we're going since you're making cookies."

"I'm not sure but I have the timer on so we can go outside on the porch. You look kind of serious. Is something up?"

"Yeah, actually it is. It has to do with why I was out

there Saturday when you fell into the water."

She nodded slightly. "Then follow me."

He pulled the door shut, then followed her down the hallway. She had on white jeans that were curled up at the ankles and black flip-flops exposing soft peach toenails. They matched the peach-toned blouse she wore. And her dark, black hair swung along her shoulder while her hips swung along with it—he yanked his gaze back up to her hair. Then focused on what was around them.

There were a couple of doors along the hall, then they entered a large, open kitchen that had an island with five stools drawn up to it on this side. A large bowl sat across the bar beside the oven. The stovetop was farther down the counter. Then, even farther down where the counter turned, was the refrigerator. The sink was on the far side of the long, large bar. The kitchen was big, open, and made for interaction.

She walked down to the refrigerator and turned toward him. "Would you like something to drink? I have tea, and lemonade, too." She smiled. "I think everyone in town is addicted to lemonade. We used to always have it. Grandpa had lemon trees over to the side near the fence. We're not the only ones—Josie Jane always has some at her store. I think she likes it as much as my gram did, which is why Grandpa had planted about ten trees. I pulled these from the six of ten that are still alive."

He saw the large bowl full of lemons. "Really, you made the lemonade?"

"Yes, I did. Couldn't help it. It was the first thing I did after we arrived."

"Then how could I resist it? Yes, I'd like a lemonade, please." She smiled, though he knew she was wondering why he was here. "How long do your cookies have?"

"Oh, they have about five minutes, so how about we stay in here for a few minutes, then I'll take them out and give some to Hazel. Then we'll go outside. And I'll give you some too."

"I've got time. No rush."

She opened the refrigerator and pulled out a clear pitcher that was nearly full of yellow lemonade.

"Looks good."

She smiled. "I think so." She opened a cabinet door and he was amazed at all the different types of glasses on the three shelves.

"Wow, that is a colorful cabinet right there."

She turned and grinned. "My gram loved to collect colorful dishes and glasses—if china had color, she loved it. All these cabinets are filled with colored dishes and I'm keeping all of them. I love them too." She pulled out two pink glasses, hesitated, then put them back and reached up to the second shelf and pulled out two pale-blue glasses. "You might like these better than pink."

He smiled. "I'll drink out of any of those pretty glasses you give me." And it was true.

She opened the cabinet next to the one she'd just opened, and it was full of colorful plates. There was a shelf of pink, then a shelf of blue, and at the top, yellow.

"You were not kidding. That's colorful. It would be cool if the cabinets had glass doors to show all that color off."

She'd pulled out a plate and smiled as she set it down next to the pad he figured she planned to set the pan of cookies. "Yes I think the same thing. It doesn't look like it would be too hard. The cabinets have that frame around the center piece, so I'm thinking that could just be removed and maybe replaced with glass. This would be a colorful kitchen then."

"I agree it would be nice and it probably wouldn't be too much trouble. I'm not a cabinet builder but it looks simple."

She pulled two small blue plates from the cabinet as the timer rang. She smiled and set the plates down, slipped her hand into a thick glove, then opened the oven and picked up the pan. He watched, seeing that she was at ease in the kitchen, more so than in the middle of the stream.

"Those smell delicious."

"These are, as you can tell, chocolate crinkle cookies that my gram loved to make for me when I was a little girl. So, I'm trying to pass that on by baking them for Hazel. And I don't know if you've heard yet, but I'm turning this into a bed-and-breakfast. It's to honor my grandparents, and her cooking and baking is going to come in handy for me. I spent many days standing on a stool beside her as she showed me how to cook."

He pictured it in his head and smiled. "She's going to love that."

"She does, but since she was in school today, she had to come home and do a little homework, so this is my treat for her. Anyway, didn't mean to get carried away. Let me take these to her and then we'll head outside." She lifted two cookies from the pan with a spatula, then added a third one to the plate, and then headed down the hall.

He heard a squeal from the little girl that made him smile and moments later, Sydney returned, smiling too. "She loves cookies," she said as she placed three cookies on a plate, then one cookie on another plate.

She handed him the plate of three cookies with a napkin tucked to the side and then handed him his glass of lemonade.

He reached for his hat on the edge of the counter and placed it on his head, then gladly took the lemonade and grinned. "Thanks. I might squeal, too."

She chuckled as she picked up the other plate and a glass of lemonade and headed for the back door. He followed her. When she reached the door, she set her drink on a small table beside it then opened the door. "No, you go first. I've got this," she said when he hesitated, wanting her to go first.

Instead, he chuckled and headed out the door. She stepped outside, reached back in, picked her glass up and set it on the table sitting outside the door, then pulled it shut. He watched as she picked her glass up and led the way to the chairs on the far side of the porch.

He grinned at her as she sat down. "You've done that a lot, I see."

Her grin was cute. "Yep, ever since I was little. Those tables were set there for a reason. We always came outside for snacks and sometimes meals, and if hands were too full, the tables came in handy."

He smiled as he sat down across from her and set his drink on the table between their chairs. Man, he hated he was about to tell her something that might upset her. He didn't want to mess up this great atmosphere. He loved it. He looked out across the yard and saw flower beds that could use some help. He knew someone in town came and mowed regularly and occasionally weeded the flower beds, but no flowers had grown here in a long time. He looked back at her and thought about the plates she liked and the way her eyes danced when she was happy. He could imagine that this was going to be one colorful yard when she got into replanting it.

Okay, get your head on straight, man.

Unable to help himself, he reached for a cookie and bit into it. "Goodness gracious," he managed to say out loud as he chewed. She laughed, and his gaze met hers. "This is awesome."

Her grin widened. "I tell you, my gram knew what she was doing."

"Well, I can tell you that you do too. My goodness. Yeah, I can tell you are going to open this bed-and-breakfast and people are going to come, and when you make them these cookies, they aren't going to want to leave." He took another bite, unable to stop himself, and it was bigger than the first. "Wow," he managed.

She had one in her hand, halfway to her lips, but was too zeroed in on watching him that she wasn't eating it. "You're really serious. You like them that much?"

"Um, yeah. My gosh. My grandma could cook and my mom can too, but this is amazing. Your grandma could have sold these. You certainly could. If the rest of the cooking you do is as good as these cookies, you need to do a cookbook. I'd buy it—not saying mine would be this good, but I'd try." He almost said, *Or you can teach me yourself,* but he managed to keep that to himself. He happened to look up, and in the window across the patio, Hazel stood, holding up her cookie and laughing. That kid had known he was going to have a good reaction when he tasted her mother's cookies. He laughed and held his cookie up; her mother followed his gaze, then grinned as she waved her hand, telling Hazel to back away from the window. Which she did with a big smile.

Sydney looked at him, her beautiful eyes sparkling. "She agrees with you. She loves them. Cute kid wanted to see your reaction, and you pleased her. Just like you did when you rescued me out of that water. You have made a fan. If I can say that."

His heart leapt in his chest, against his ribs. "She's adorable, and I can only say again that I'm glad I was there. I know you would have been okay as long as you didn't hit your head on something and gone into the water unconscious. But anyway, I'm glad I was there and now get to see Hazel smile and you, too, and I get to enjoy this cookie. Or cookies, because I can tell you I'm going to eat every one of them." That got another grin from her.

She took a bite and the white sugar left a mark on her upper lip.

He smiled. "See? Good. And—" He leaned forward before he could stop himself, and lifted his finger to her lip and wiped the sugar off. But his fingers stilled as he touched her and she froze.

Her eyes widened, and she sucked in a breath.

What am I doing?

"Sorry." His gaze lingered on her lips as he pulled his fingers away. "Didn't mean to do that." *Fix this.* "I probably have it all over my mouth, too." And he was serious.

Thank goodness he'd said the right thing, because she met his gaze finally and smiled.

"Actually, it's all over your top lip."

He laughed and reached for the napkin and wiped his lips, and yes, the dust was clearly visible on the pale-yellow napkin. "I think you knew that would happen." He was thankful it had and given him some relief from the mistake he'd made of touching her when he shouldn't have.

"I thought it might."

"No matter what, they are still the best thing I've eaten in my lifetime. Just don't tell my mom."

"Your secret is safe with me."

They stared at each other, and he suddenly knew it was time to get to why he'd come. This was not the place he needed to be staring at this beautiful woman and knowing what he felt was wrong.

"So, I guess we need to get to why I came. I don't want to mess up enjoying these wonderful cookies but I need to tell you..." He looked at the cookie, then back at her.

She was still watching him.

"Obviously what you are here to tell me is not good. So now you have my curiosity going. What's going on?"

"Saturday…" He set his cookie back on the plate and dusted his hand off on the napkin, then leaned forward, placing his elbows on his knees so he was closer to her. He didn't want Hazel to hear anything he said, or if she was near the window, he didn't want her to maybe read his lips. Unlikely but he was taking no chances. He started over. "Saturday, I was out there and it wasn't just because I was exploring the pastures. It was because I'm pretty positive we've had a mountain lion out there."

She dropped her cookie into her lap she was so stunned, and his heart fell to the ground.

CHAPTER NINE

Sydney stared at Dustin. Her heart thundered up into her throat. "You mean when we went down there, a mountain lion was there?" She forced the question out.

"Yes, that's what I suspect. And I had come down to see if I could find any signs of it that might prove my suspicion right. See, we found two dead cows a week apart. The last one was about three weeks ago. They were healthy cows, not sick and weak. Because we don't come out here every day, they'd been dead for several days, but coyotes had been there and they don't waist time eating slow or alone. Their footprints were the only ones around. My suspicion went up immediately but there was no one living here, so I didn't get too worried. They tend to come out at night, but when I heard you had moved in, I got worried and decided to check it out.

"They don't attack people usually. California has some problems with it but not Texas. Not so far. Still, I was worried about y'all being here. So, I came out to search for signs and found you in the water. Not what I was expecting, but I can say I think I was put there to help you and very glad I was."

"Me too."

His insides nearly busted with happiness at her words, but he forced himself to focus on his warning to her. "I told my brothers what I was alarmed about and immediately they wanted to come out and search this morning. Knowing you two had moved in here put their alert system on high, too. We've been out there all day and found nothing. Anyway, I knew I had to come tell you why I was out there."

She had set her plate on the table beside her lemonade. Her hands were wrapped together, and her eyes were wide with fright. He could tell her thoughts were running. "So that means if y'all aren't here much and there hasn't been anyone living in this house, that that animal could think this was a safe roaming area. You're telling me we have to watch out."

"Yeah, that's exactly why I'm here. I needed to let you know why going down there by that river right now isn't a good idea. And I know Hazel loves it down there. I love it too, so, I understand her love of it. But me and all the fellas in my family are on it. We loved your grandparents very much and we're grateful we were able to buy the property, but I—we think you and Hazel deserve to roam that land as much as y'all want to. And the cattle don't mind, as long as you're aware to watch out for snakes—that is important too.

"But the fact that there could possibly be a mountain lion out there that we don't know what to expect he'll do is not good. They do move a lot and my hope is that it's already moved on, but I have to be sure about that. The fact that we found nothing today that suggests it's still around is good. Still, I'd like you to be aware and cautious. They all agreed I needed to come alert you about what's going on."

She reached out, to his startled surprise, and wrapped her soft hand around his two cupped hands and squeezed gently.

Rampant shots of fire instantly roared through him,

and was alarming in some ways. It was things he didn't need to feel for her. He looked into her eyes, her beautiful emerald eyes.

"Thank you for telling me. Thank you for being there the other day but…thank you for this especially because I'll know to put extra eyes on my daughter. She does like to play outside. As the summer arrives, she'll be out here more. She has an adventurous spirit and I'm hoping…." She squeezed his hand tighter.

It wasn't a hand holding his out of attraction, but a hand gripping his as she coped with fear racing through her and gratefulness that he'd come and warned her. And that was all it was.

He gave her the moment to come up with the words she'd been saying. If he'd had a free hand, he'd have cupped hers, but she was clasping his tightly, so he nodded. "I promise, if I have to start spending the night out there on that ridge, I'll do it. Don't be afraid to ask me anything. You're alerted, so if you see a footprint or eaten carcass, let me know. Be on the lookout. You can get out there and work out there in what I suspect is going to be a beautiful yard. Making this bed-and-breakfast even more charming. So I have a feeling that you're going to be out there moving around, and if that mountain lion is out there, he's going to stay away. I just want you to be cautious and don't let her go down there alone."

"Thank you," she said, breathless as her gaze dropped from his to her hand. Then, as if realizing what she was doing, she suddenly released her hand and yanked it back to her lap. "Thank you. I know I've said that a lot. But it's only me and Hazel now. My family lives in the city and loves it. So thank you for looking out for us. I appreciate it very much."

He pulled his hands back and sat up. "I'm glad to be here as a friend to help you in any way that I can. And all my brothers and my two cousins who live with us are in agreement that we're here for you. We loved your granddad and your grandmother. But we were closer to Johnny. That man—he loved cattle and animals, and when your grandma got sick and he sold the land to us, we would sometimes bring a horse here so he could come ride with us to round them up. He really enjoyed it. So, as far as we are concerned, that land is as much yours and that sweet girl of yours to roam on. And we're going to make sure that gets to happen."

Tears—he could see them but she blinked them away as she gave him a smile, a touching smile that dug deep with its gentleness.

"It's like my grandpa knew we needed to be here. He could have split this place between all of us, and we would have had to sell it. But he knew I needed a place to come after losing Nelson, though it took me a bit to know it was here that we needed to be. But he knew in his heart of hearts that here in this wonderful small town and this home was where my heart needed to be. And where my baby needs to grow up. And he also knew there were special people like you and your brothers and all those in town who would surround us with love. So, thank you. I'm grateful. Very grateful."

"I'm glad we're here. And this is my ranch business card," he pulled the card out of his shirt pocket that he'd put there just for her. "If you need anything please call me.

She took it and stared at it for a moment then looked

at him once more and nodded. "Another thank you for this. But hopefully I won't need to call you."

* * *

They were walking down the hall moments after their talk. She had put his uneaten cookies in a small plastic bag and had placed four others in there beside it. She'd handed it to him and he noticed she'd made sure her fingers didn't touch his. That motion had something in the back of his head tingling. He shut that thought down and didn't even let it come alive. Then he'd headed down the hall, toward the front door and his escape. He assured her he would alert her if they discovered anything else. As they neared the door, Hazel barreled down the hallway, making him smile at her energy.

"Okay, so when, when are we going to go across the log?"

"Oh, ah," he muttered as his gaze went to her mom. What did he say? They hadn't even talked about that.

Her mother smiled at her daughter. "Well, I'm not sure, but only when and if Dustin can go with us. You understand that, right? Never do you go down there without him. Do you understand?"

Hazel looked at her, then him, and then nodded solemnly. "Okay, yes, I promise I won't do that. Mama, you look worried. I won't do something to make you cry. I won't. I promise. But can we go?"

Her gaze locked on his. "When your mom says yes, we'll go. Any time." He looked at Sydney's face and saw the struggle there.

"Obviously, today is getting late, so it's not a good day. And I hear y'all are having a wedding Saturday for Genna and West, and this morning she invited us," she looked at her daughter then back at him, "to their wedding. So, Saturday wouldn't be good because we're all going to a wedding. So, maybe Sunday. That gives us several days."

He knew the way she said it that this was to give him several days to catch a mountain lion, if possible. He smiled. "Yes, that gives us some days. We are getting ready for the wedding, and I have to go try on a tuxedo tomorrow. Well, just a tux jacket. We're wearing our jeans and boots because we're cowboys—you know how that goes. But we are going to wear the tuxedo jacket because of Genna and the fact that our first brother is getting married. My mom and dad are thrilled."

He chuckled, because it was so very true. "I mean, they are usually traveling all over the place but they are so thrilled and excited and are at the ranch, caught up in getting everything ready. They're hosting our dinner on Friday night and it's going to be a great evening. Then, on Saturday, that sweet Genna is going to become my sister-in-law. And I have to say that the fact that she came from who knows where—the woman has practically traveled the world with her parents and then out of a memory from her mom talking about coming here when she was a girl, she moves here and claims our town as home—it's amazing. And," he chuckled, "not that she ever had any goats, but the strangest thing was that she loved them. She loved to watch cute videos of them online, and lo and behold, she met my brother, and he loves them, too. It was like a match made in heaven.

"We all enjoy them because my grandma raised them. Her family always raised goats and hogs and sheep, along with fruit and vegetables on a farm. My granddaddy raised cows and horses, and when they met and fell in love, they combined those two loves. We were raised among cattle and goats mostly. We all live in different cabins on the ranch, and plan to build houses when we're ready. But West loved the home Grandpa and Grandma lived in and asked early on if he could have it one day." He paused. "I'm probably boring you both."

"No, you're not," Hazel blurted. "Does your brother raise goats now?"

He smiled. "Yes. Since he loves those goats as much as Grandma did, they left the house to him. He lives there now, and he does the books for the ranch and helps with the cattle when he's ready to get out of the office. But he loves watching out for Grandma's goats and raises a lot of them. Right there in the front yard of the house and barn. And that's where him and Genna are going to live. Hey, you two will have to come out and see the goats. Would you like that?" he asked Hazel.

She beamed up at him, then at her mom. "This man knows stuff." She looked back at him. "Yes, I want to see the goats. When can I see them?"

"Well, me and your mom will talk about it. I'm actually going to be taking care of the goats while they're on their honeymoon. So, as of Saturday, the moment they get married and leave for the airport, those goats are going to be in my hands. That means I'll be out there a lot, feeding and watering them. I can just tell you right now you're welcome any time. You might be wanting more to come out and watching all ages of goats climbing on all kinds of crazy things in their yard rather than walking across that tree.

"Those goats can climb anything. You should see all these big ole barrels stacked on top of each other— they're locked together so they won't roll on top of anyone. They love it. We have two donkeys that they love to jump on and off of." She grinned and he did too. "The donkeys love it. They let them have all the jumping fun they want. They are just good old fellas. But I can tell you—" His gaze went to Sydney. She was looking at him as if he'd just spoken miracle words. It made him feel good. "—once you get out there, she may not want to leave."

"Well, I have to say, that you have enthralled me too. I remember them from all those years ago, though I only saw them a few times when my grandpa would go out for various reasons to see your grandpa. But I can't wait to see them again."

They hadn't seen each other during those times, either he wasn't at their house, or he'd been so busy on the ranch with his dad working cattle that he hadn't been looking for visitors. "Yeah, maybe Sunday, instead of thinking about walking across that log, y'all can come out while I'm feeding them. What do you say?"

She looked at her daughter, who was nodding. "Yes, I can't wait. They have little bitty ones, with little horns sticking up? And big ones too?"

"They sure do. Some are really small and would be like holding a puppy. They have them in all sizes, and they all love to jump and play. Matter of fact, you might not want to get down on the ground with them too much because they'll have you rolling around with them. And you can help me feed them, too."

She laughed. "I love it." Then she lunged at him, throwing her arms around his leg again and holding on tight. "You have made me happy. Real happy. I can't wait to see the goats."

That look on her face had caused his heart to clutch. He was still thinking about it as he drove away, and also the way that her mother watched him. But that look in her eye he couldn't take for granted or put hope on, because she wasn't ready and he wasn't going to pressure that. If he did, all he would do was take the chance of pushing her away. So this, for him, was not an act of kindness, because he was crazy about Hazel and her mom. It was just an act of doing something that made him smile and feel alive inside in ways he'd never felt before. Giving him feelings like he'd never wanted to lose.

Oh yeah, once in college, he'd thought he was in love and he'd been done wrong, and because of that, he'd closed the door—no, he'd slammed the door on ever letting someone get close to his heart. But, unbelievably, all Sydney had to do was look at him once and he'd forgotten all about that gal in college and any kind of decisions he'd made on never opening his heart again.

But, as hard as he was hoping her heart would open up and she could love again, it was not something he was going to push. He was just going to be there for these two, however they needed him.

And that idea made him smile inside.

CHAPTER TEN

The day after the meeting with Dustin about the mountain lion, Sydney dropped a chattering little girl off at her new school. And then she drove back to town and this time went straight to Josie Jane's Wash and Repeat. Josie Jane was at the counter toward the middle of the store, and there were all the places to sit that she remembered from when she was younger. And at one of them, at barely eight o'clock in the morning, sat the tall, lanky Millie, who owned a store on the other side of the street. They both smiled enthusiastically at her.

"Good morning. We're sitting here talking about the next dance we're going to hold in town," Josie Jane said.

Millie patted the flowery, very well-padded chair

next to hers. "We're really excited about having it."

"Yes, we are. We loved everything about the last dance. And we have heard that you're opening your place, just as we hoped you would, as a bed-and-breakfast. That makes us even more excited. We were going to come see you and ask when you think it's going to be opened. We could plan the dance around it, as a celebratory thing. We know you'll be booked. You know, we'd like for you to be able to come to the dances too."

"Yes, hopefully you'll be able to lock up and come to the dance and bring your little girl and y'all have fun."

She smiled at them, and thought about that. "I'm glad y'all are so excited. I am, too, actually. That's what I came to talk to y'all about, and you've pointed out a good thing. I'll need to make it to where I can come…hmm, okay, every door in the house can have its own key, with a key to the front door of the house on the key ring. Then I can lock up and come. Hopefully everyone who books with me will be trustworthy people that I don't have to worry about stealing some of my grandparents' things that I love so much. This gives me some good things to think about and check into. Yesterday, I called a place in Marble Falls, where Jasmine lives right now. She suggested some places her relatives used to do updates to their homes. So they're coming out to give me estimates on the rooms I need painted. They said they have plenty of people and can get to it quickly.

"So that would be good, but by the way y'all talk, I may be booked up at first without even putting out an ad. According to Jasmine, her mom will fill my place up, at least the first time, and then word will get out. I'm not worried about customers. With Nelson's insurance and what my grandparents left to me and all my family that I don't actually have to have the income. I just want it to be a success and benefit the town, and so I'm really excited about it. It gives me something wonderful, other than my sweet daughter, to think about. And she is excited too. So, here I am. What else do you think I need to do? I hear all of your stores are amazing, so I'm going to start shopping around for neat things to update with where I need to. I'd love them to come from places in town."

Josie Jane grinned hugely. "I think that is a wonderful, wonderful idea. You just look around, and if you see something you want, I'll discount it. I'm so thrilled about you being here—I want to help."

"Me too," Millie said, her smile wide. "This town means everything to me. And I'm excited to see everyone enthusiastic about what we're doing. We are going to throw a wonderful dance. And I have some new ideas. Since it's still summertime, and people are actively getting out and about, we're thinking of adding something to it. Like maybe a petting zoo for the kids. From what I hear, those Buckley cowboys have a wonderful goat farm, and Genna talks about how much she loves watching them play and petting them. Me and Josie Jane were talking about that, and we think we're going to ask them to provide them to a petting zoo. It won't just be a dance but a day of fun. And we'll have our stores open and refreshment places open. Even though Red and Ruby's place will be open and busy, I don't think there's any way they could feed the crowd we're anticipating."

"So true," Josie Jane agreed. "What do you think?"

Sydney had started grinning halfway through the long statement. "I can tell you that Hazel will love it. She just found out yesterday about all the goats, and we're actually going out Sunday to see them. Hazel is totally thrilled. Therefore, I have to say what you two are saying would delight her and all the kids. After Sunday, I can give you a thumbs-up, thumbs-down, but I have a feeling it's going to be a two-thumbs-up report on our experience."

"Wonderful," Josie Jane said in a drawn-out drawl as her gaze locked with Millie's for a moment.

Sydney wasn't sure what she was seeing, so she ignored it. "I'm contemplating putting a small pen for a couple of goats out at my place and also getting a dog. If she loves goats as much as I think she will, they would give her something to take care of and love on. And my customers might also. My B&B might also have a sort of petting area or a place to just sit and watch them play on their playground inside the fenced area. I haven't said anything to Hazel yet, but I know she'll be excited. Anyway, that's where my mind has been going ever since Dustin invited us out."

"Dustin came by and invited y'all to do that?" Josie Jane asked.

Sydney studied their bright, inquisitive eyes. "Well, yes, y'all know he pulled me out of the water—thank goodness. I found out that there was more to the story about why he was out there that day. He came by yesterday and told me. Actually, though I didn't see them on the other side of the wooded ravine, all the Buckley men were out there before he came by to see me. They were looking for a mountain lion that they suspect killed two of their cattle late last month. That's why he came by yesterday, to tell me this."

"A mountain lion? Oh goodness," Josie Jane gasped.

Millie held her hand up. "But wait, you said late last month, so that's about three weeks or so. That's good. He might be gone now. Most likely he is."

They both looked at the rodeo champion.

"How do you know that?" Josie Jane asked.

"Yes, how? That's what Dustin is hoping for, but he wants to make sure so me and Hazel don't get hurt."

Millie waved her hand and settled back in her chair.

"My dad and grandpa were hunters. They loved to travel on hunting expeditions, and they talked about it. And one of the things they talked about was mountain lions. They live alone and move about most of the time. Their range is an average of five to a hundred square miles. And just so you know, one square mile is equal to six hundred and forty acres. So they travel a lot."

Josie Jane and Sydney looked at each other in amazement. Then Sydney looked back at the incredible cowgirl, who obviously knew more than just horses. "Maybe Dustin needs to talk to you. He said he did research and that he thinks it's probably moved on but because the attacks took place at least three weeks before we moved in, he just felt like he needed to make sure."

Millie smiled. "He's a good man, that one. And I'll be glad to talk to him but I have a feeling he's dug deep in his research. The good thing that I'll make sure he knows is that every mountain lion marks his space and he's the only one that roams it. Unless he's mating and that's only for a very few days…no more than ten, I believe." She laughed. "That means, maybe, I'm not sure about this, but if he stayed in the area a few days longer than usual that maybe he was mating. I think mating season is December to…March. Therefore, with the dates they're looking at, this isn't that time of year. Anyway, you can rest fairly easy that this big ghost cat, puma, cougar, or mountain screamer—just a few of the names of these golden cats—has moved on. They're known by over forty names." She grinned after her long, interesting, and positive declaration.

"Goodness gracious, Millie. I'm in awe." Josie Jane then laughed. "Lady, you need to talk more. I'm totally enthralled. And relieved for you, Sydney."

Sydney felt the same way. This woman was like a walking encyclopedia and obviously everyone in town had no idea. "You've given me much relief, and I'll tell Dustin. But, okay, I can't help it, what else do you know about them?"

"Yes, tell us. I'll feel super smart after this." Josie Jane laughed loudly, her green eyes sparkling.

Millie chuckled and waved her hands again. "I have a great memory, so now you know. Okay, so…the only wild cat bigger than them is a jaguar. They can run about forty miles an hour—no, forty-five miles an hour. And to help you, they don't attack humans hardly at all. It does happen, but not much here in Texas, where they have a lot of room to hide out and avoid us. Let me think for a minute…"

She looked thoughtful, as if rolling through that incredible mind of hers. "They don't often eat cattle but sometimes. And if there are a lot of coyotes or wolves around, the food they've killed doesn't last long. And we have plenty of those around here. Coyotes, for certain. So that right there might have been the deal. He killed the cow and ate some, then the coyotes moved in."

"Yes, that's what Dustin said—there were no paw prints, only coyotes."

She smiled. "There you go. As you can tell, I was a little infatuated with them, listening to my dad and grandpa talk. And besides riding my horse growing up, I liked to explore things, so I read a lot of books. Because of them, I studied up on mountain lions and they really appreciated it and asked me a lot of questions." She grinned. "My memory was better than theirs." Her eyes sparkled and they all laughed.

This woman was incredible. Sydney laughed so hard, she had settled back in her chair and her arms were wrapped over her stomach. "You have truly made my day. Really. And hopefully when I tell Dustin this, it will help him too. I may call him and have him drop by so you can show him your amazing brain in person."

"Yes, in person, because she truly is amazing," Josie Jane said, grinning widely.

"I'd be happy to talk to him. Now, tell us more about what y'all will be doing with Dustin."

She smiled. How could she not say more considering this amazingly smart woman with a memory that was stunning had been so open?

"Well, he's going to be showing Hazel the goats and letting her play with all of them. She's going to love it. And I'll enjoy seeing her joy. But that's all we'll be doing." She hoped she didn't have to point-blank tell them that there was nothing romantic going on. Thankfully, the two looked at each other, then at her, and nodded.

She wasn't sure whether she was supposed to

believe that nod or not, but she couldn't ask them whether they were serious or contemplating something in their amazing brains. And she certainly wasn't going to admit that to her startlement, surprise, and shock last night, deep in the night when she'd been lying there awake instead of sleeping, her brain had locked on Dustin. But it was his niceness that her thoughts dwelled on. It was as if he knew her child meant everything to her and that her child needed some things in her life that reminded her of her times with her dad.

She forced down the hint of emotion. Hazel's beloved dad wasn't here to give her those moments and though she was not attracted in that way to him, despite the softening of her feelings for him, it was almost as if he understood them and had volunteered to step in. She knew it came from him diving into that water and saving her. Then helping her up that incline to the arms of her sweet Hazel. And then her little darling's words. It was just as if that moment had tied them together.

As much as she didn't want to have someone step into her darling husband's spot, she knew that Hazel had a humongous, open heart and was seeking the attention.

And she couldn't completely stand in the way of that. Oh yes, she could if she thought there was something horrible about him, but as far as she could see, even in the eyes of people when they heard what had happened, she could see only delight that he'd been there for her. No one had anything bad to say about the man.

And that was good. It gave her security in knowing that she could still pick a good man out of a slew of them. Only this good man wasn't for her. He was to help her daughter keep moving forward and not be so enclosed in the loss of her daddy as she was in losing her husband. Opening up some for Hazel could be good for both of them. This was their new beginning. And again, like her grandpa had probably thought when he left this wonderful home to her, was that everything about this town was what they needed. She doubted he knew she was going to fall into the stream and get rescued, but he had been a very smart, wise man, and she loved that Dustin said such nice things about him.

She loved that they'd brought him a horse so he could go herding cattle when he felt like it after they'd bought his ranch land. She knew he'd loved his life as a cattleman and loved her grandma enough to give it all up and be there for her as that horrible disease had taken her. Sydney forever loved him for that. And even if he'd been contemplating putting Grandma in a nursing home as a last resort, he'd managed to hire some help so he could keep her home. And then she'd gone quickly, and he'd worked hard to start a happy life over here in the town they loved. And part of that was because of those Buckley men taking him into their cattle checks when he wanted. She was so grateful to them for that.

Now this one was helping her with her sweet Hazel. The little one who worked so hard to make her mother not worry about her.

She had to do what helped her little girl and made her smile and not worry about her. It was time she tried not to cry anymore. It had been three years, and she could feel Nelson beside her, urging her forward. Forward for their daughter's sake, she could do that. And that's why they'd come here. She'd just never thought someone like Dustin could help fill the gap left in her daughter's world, where her daddy couldn't be anymore.

"So, I'm excited they are going to come and paint soon, and I'll be ready—well, I have to check into any permits I might need but I think that wouldn't take too long. You ladies get ready—I should be ready in at least three weeks. Jasmine's mom has assured me that she will have my place filled up whenever we have the party. So we're going to make her day. She is an amazing woman, and I'm really glad to meet her sweet daughter who…" She paused, having almost said *had something in her past too* but she kept her mouth shut. Her thoughts on things like that didn't need to come out. She didn't need to speculate what was wrong with someone. Time would tell on that. But one thing she knew: this was the place to heal and start over.

CHAPTER ELEVEN

It had been a busy week. Dustin had called Sydney to see how they were doing, and he'd almost blurted out an invitation to last night's dinner before the wedding tonight. But he had come to his senses and put himself in his place and hadn't made the wrong move of asking her out.

They were going tomorrow to see the goats, and they were going as friends. It was all about helping Hazel have some fun. He knew that watching her sweet girl have fun would also help Sydney relax and have a day of enjoyment. And, personally, he couldn't wait to see joy and fun in her eyes because one thing those goats could do was make you laugh.

So, now he stood at the front of the area beside West. Genna hadn't had any women her age she knew well enough because they'd traveled so much that she'd never really made a close friend. So she was going to walk the aisle alone to stand beside her best friend and the man she would love from now and for always.

Dustin smiled, thinking about that. They were barely a year apart in age and he was standing here beside him because West said it was his talking him down the night of the town dance when he was about to mess up that had helped him, and he wanted Dustin there because in helping him, he'd helped Genna too.

It had touched Dustin and he'd agreed. Though all of his brothers and his cousins were close, there was no denying that through their years growing up, he and West had always seemed to talk the same language when it came to things that mattered.

He was glad to stand here with his brother and his bride, but as he looked out across the guests, he realized he would be glad to get a glimpse of Sydney during the ceremony. So many of the townsfolk had come to celebrate, and they were going to party after the vows were shared, the rings were placed on fingers, and the kiss after the preacher pronounced them husband and wife. Everyone was here to share the joy and dance the night away. This was a good excuse to introduce her to his parents, like he wanted to do.

He scanned the audience now. He'd been in the back with West and the preacher, so he hadn't seen Sydney and Hazel come in. His other brothers had been the ones escorting everyone to their seats. Now that he and his soon-to-be-married brother, along with the preacher, were in their places, he could see where she was. And then he found them. They sat toward the middle on the outside edge of the left side. She'd placed Hazel on the outside chair so if she needed to lean out and see what was going on, she could. He knew that because as his gaze found theirs, she did exactly that—leaned out, grinning at him, and waved.

His own smile instantly reacted, and he lifted his hand to his chest and curled his fingers in hello to her.

She grinned real big, then turned to her mom. He could hear the words, as could everyone else. "He waved at me, Mama."

Sydney chuckled as she leaned down and obviously told Hazel she didn't need to talk so loud. He figured this because when they finished talking, Hazel leaned out and grinned as she stuck her finger in front of her lips, as if telling him to be quiet.

He almost laughed but maintained it as a smile, then felt the nudge of his brother. He glanced at him; West's lips were hitched up in a grin, obviously having seen his and Hazel's exchange. It was then that Dustin glanced around the room and saw all the people who sat near Hazel and Sydney. All those who had for certain seen what was going on. Millie and Josie Jane sat across the aisle, in exactly the same row as Hazel and Sydney, and they were grinning. Ruby and Red sat behind them and had obviously seen everything, too, because they both grinned.

Oh boy. He was supposed to be really happy right now, and he was happy about knowing Hazel had sought him out to wave at and grin. But there was the worry—*what if everyone started getting ideas?* There was no denying that for him, he would ask Sydney to marry him in a heartbeat—the realization hit him hard and strong as he realized without doubt how much he loved her.

At that very moment, he wished he could trade places with his brother and watch Sydney walk up that aisle to him. But she'd been there and done that, and obviously been extremely happy until the moment it had ended. The moment her husband died. Dustin knew there was no way that he could even step across that line—he took a mental fist and socked himself in the head for even standing there and thinking such a thing. He had to remember to not do anything like that again. Those actions would make people think that there was something brewing between him and Sydney.

It didn't matter how much he wanted it. He loved Sydney. He hadn't known her for very long but he had never in his life felt what he felt for her. He tried not to look at her but he did, and she was looking at him and quickly looked down. But even in that brief moment, his heart had shot up, down, then bounced from his ribs in front to his back. He'd messed up. *Tomorrow. He just had to think about tomorrow.* When it would just be the three of them playing with the goats. Just them and no one there to watch them or to assume things and get something riled up and wrong.

Not that he thought those three nice ladies and Red, the man, would actually do anything to hurt Sydney. But he didn't want them to accidentally pressure her. And he didn't want the pressure either. He did not want rumors to start, and he knew Sydney wouldn't like it if they did.

The wedding march started, and everyone stood and turned slightly to see Genna and her stepfather come into the doorway. She looked amazing. His brother was marrying a beautiful woman. Her pretty, dark hair had been curled; half of it had been lifted up from her shoulders in curls, and the small hints of red in her hair sparkled in the lights. She wasn't wearing the...the...veil. His brain was stumbling around. Not everyone wore them but her hair was so beautiful, there was no need for her to wear one. And many women didn't. He liked veils, but he didn't care whether his bride wore one or not. The only person he wanted to marry was Sydney, and she could wear whatever she wanted to wear as she walked down that aisle to him.

Sydney would be beautiful with or without a veil— He yanked his brain away from that, and watched Genna start down the aisle. Her dress flowed behind her, and she was breathtaking and looked so happy with her gleaming smile. He glanced at his brother. West looked captivated; he could see it in his eyes and the way they glittered with moisture, he was so enchanted by the love of his life walking toward him. Dustin could understand why.

Actually, Dustin envied him. He was happy for him and wondered which of the Buckleys would fall in love and get married next. In his heart of hearts, he wished it was him. But as Genna made it to the front of the aisle and her stepdad handed her off to West, Dustin's gaze met sweet Sydney's, and instead of looking away for a moment…his heart raced as he saw emotion there in her gaze. Emotion that tore at him. Then she blinked and looked away.

And then his gaze met Hazel's. Her eyes beamed, and she grinned at him. He couldn't tear his eyes from the little kid as she leaned into the aisle and gave him a thumbs-up.

* * *

Sydney sat still, watching West and Genna say their

vows to each other. Her heart ached as a memory of her and Nelson exchanging vows surfaced. But she had been caught as Genna had come up the aisle with her gaze settled on Dustin.

She hadn't even realized she was looking at him while she was thinking of marrying Nelson. But she saw in his eyes a look of pure...*love?*

She only ever had that look from one other man, her sweet Nelson. She'd never wanted that look again. She'd never wanted what was pounding in her heart suddenly as she watched Genna and West trade rings, each slipping their ring on the other's finger. And then the preacher pronounced them husband and wife. Her chest hurt as he told West he could kiss his bride...

Oh, how she remembered that moment with Nelson. As those words were being said, she realized once again she was looking at Dustin. *Why?*

She yanked her gaze away and stared at her trembling hands. *What was wrong with her?*

Her baby was sitting beside her, and she had to get a hold of herself—get hold of this craziness gripping her. She would never again go through the pain she'd suffered when she'd lost her beloved husband. She couldn't. It still hurt too much. Her insides trembled and her words, though only to herself, were words accompanied by tears. She sucked in a deep breath. She had decided she was moving forward. This wasn't forward. She focused on her determination. She'd been feeling joy since being here and felt so happy seeing the way Hazel was embracing it. And tomorrow...oh goodness, they were going with Dustin to play with goats.

Little goats, medium goats, and big goats. She could just see the joy that was going to be written all over Hazel's face. And her words of exclamation were going to carry the ring of joy. Oh yes, she'd been on pretty wonderful vacations with her young Hazel and her daddy. And that child loved those trips. It had been a while since she'd enjoyed herself so much. But she knew, with as much excitement as she'd shown when Dustin had told her about those goats, that she was going to see her darling girl as excited as she'd been all those years ago when she'd shared something special with her daddy. He'd been gone three years, so Hazel had been five when they lost him—when the burning building had fallen on top of him and burned their hearts up with him.

She felt a wave of dizziness. A surge of longing. Oh, how she missed those wonderful moments they'd shared. The love that had surrounded them… And though she didn't want it to, her gaze lifted and found Dustin.

He was looking at his brother as he lifted the hand of his bride and announced that he and his sweet Genna had done it. Then they'd started down the aisle, hand in hand, to the clapping and cheers of everyone. Dustin gave them a few steps, then followed them down.

But as he neared them, Hazel jumped out into the aisle and threw her arms around his hips and hugged him tight.

Tears welled in Sydney's eyes.

"You did a great job," Hazel exclaimed.

Dustin leaned down without looking at her and gave her daughter a hug. "I was there supporting my brother and my new sister-in-law. And I'm looking forward to seeing you tomorrow."

"We're coming to the dance!" Hazel squealed. "Aren't you going to be at the dance?"

His gaze lifted up and touched Sydney's, then jerked back down to Hazel. "Yes. I'll be there. We have to be there for my brother, and I need to celebrate his happy day. Are you sure you're going to be there?" His gaze went to Sydney and she knew the question was directed to her.

"I am," Hazel declared. "My mama promised me that we can go, and she said there was going to be some good desserts and dancing. Hey, will you dance with me?"

He chuckled, and Sydney almost started crying. Hazel used to love to dance with her daddy.

"Sure I will, if your mom says it's okay."

Hazel looked up at her.

"Of course you can. You always loved to dance." Her voice nearly broke with emotion.

Hazel spun around and threw her arms around his neck. "I used to always dance with my daddy. This will be the first time…" Her words stumbled, and she leaned back and cupped Dustin's face with her palms. "I think it's good that my first dance since my daddy had to leave will be with you. You're a great guy." Her words trembled and she looked up at her mom, and her hazel eyes sparkled with tears. "It's going to be fun, Mama. It is."

Dear God, stop my tears. She shook herself internally and swiped away the tears. "Yes, darling. You're going to have fun. And I can guarantee you that your daddy will be watching from heaven and smiling."

Dustin looked up at her and, oh goodness, he had tears in his eyes.

She forced herself to be strong. "She can dance. She's good. She knows the two-step and some of the faster dances. They used to do them, and they were wonderful."

He stood up and patted her sweet daughter on the head, and touched her cheek. "Okay, darlin'. I need to go and take some pictures with the family. And then I'll come find you."

Hazel smiled up at him. "I'll be waiting."

And then he looked at Sydney. "See you in a few minutes."

She nodded and then he walked away, and she managed not to watch him.

CHAPTER TWELVE

Genna walked out of the barn literally walking on air as her husband had his arm now wrapped around her waist and all their friends and family cheered them on. Delight and happiness like she'd never felt before had seized her. She smiled as they headed to the area that had been set up for their photos after the service. They'd taken some before but now, these were when they were actually husband and wife. Truly, happily, and forevermore West and Genna Buckley.

They reached the spot and smiled at each other as they waited for their family to gather round them. Her mother and her stepdad were grinning from ear to ear as they hurried toward them. She was suddenly almost crying as she threw herself into their arms. Then she yanked her sweet new husband into the crowd and they all hugged.

"I'm so glad to call you my son-in-law," her stepfather said.

Her heart nearly cinched as she saw the genuine love and sincerity of the man who had raised her most of her life as he opened his heart to the man she loved. She cupped his cheek, tears forming in her eyes, and she smiled up at him. She loved this man, her father. Oh, how she wished she'd known her real father but she hadn't, and yet this man had stepped into that spot and given her his whole love of a father to a daughter while he loved her mother like she so deserved to be loved. She saw the tears in her mother's eyes as she saw how Genna was tenderly touching the man she'd trusted to love her and raise Genna.

"Thank you for walking me down the aisle. It was perfect and meant to be. And thank you for loving my mother like you do. And making her smile like that." She looked at West, who was taking in the scene. "If I can make this wonderful man smile like you've made my mom and my mom has made you smile, then I know he'll be happy, and that will make me happy."

Her mother now had tears flowing, and they were going to have photos taken; she dabbed with tissues, then stopped and smiled through the tears. "Oh my goodness, I'm going to look terrible in those pictures, but what you're saying is so beautiful. Oh, how I love all of you. And West, we are so thrilled to have you as part of our family now. And we're thrilled to be a part of your family, too. I love your mom and dad. They are just great."

West smiled. "I love y'all. You gave me this wonderful gift of your daughter, and let me just tell you that you're beautiful without your makeup. These pictures are going to be memories of this moment when we combined our families and how happy it made us."

In that moment, his mom and dad—who had obviously been standing near—walked up, and his mom had tears in her eyes as she wrapped her arms around Genna's mom. "We love your daughter. And I don't know about you, but I can't wait to see what our grandbabies are going to look like."

Genna loved the look on their faces as they both started to giggle with happiness. Genna laughed, too, and so did the two dads. She looked at West. "I think that's a message that we need to get busy."

West grinned and pulled her close. "Darlin', I'm ready whenever you are. I can't even imagine life ever again without you, but just to think about a whole assortment of little ones who look like you….oh boy, I can't wait."

Suddenly, Ryder whooped then chuckled. "Okay, fellas, West is getting this party started, and we're evidently going to have lots of kids romping around pretty soon."

Genna laughed and saw that all the guys had gathered around them, all grinning. Even Dustin, though he looked a little sad—and she thought she knew why. Then the hugs began and, yes, the pictures were filled with tears and joy. And she was going to love them. And afterward, she got hugs from all of her new brothers-in-law. When Dustin came up to give her a hug, she put her hand on his cheek. "You look happy for us but somehow you look sad, too. I just want to tell you that I have an idea about what might be going on. I just want to tell you to hold on. And I believe you're going to find happiness."

She saw the emotion fill his eyes; then he gave her

a kiss on the cheek.

"I'm going to go in. I have a little girl waiting to dance with me, and I can't let her down."

Genna smiled at him and watched him walk away. She hoped and prayed things were going to go his way.

* * *

The open tent was huge and filled with the lowering sun. The tables were beautiful and the flowers were perfect. Thankfully there were restrooms nearby, in a very nice barn with large group bathrooms that must have been built to handle the cattle sales crowd, and worked great for parties and weddings. She had brought Hazel in and taken deep breaths while Hazel was in a stall. She looked at herself in the mirror and took more deep breaths.

She had to get hold of herself; she could not get so close to crying again. Tonight, her daughter was going to have fun. She was going to dance with the man she was letting fill the part of her heart that couldn't be filled in the future by her father. But she gave her father all of her heart and was able to accept both her daddy's love

151

and this completely obvious love that she held for Dustin Buckley. Sydney sniffed and glared at herself in the mirror. *Do not cry*, she mouthed at herself. She'd said she was done.

Then Hazel came out of the stall, straightening her dress and smiling.

"Okay, Mama, you ready? I'm going to go dance, and I'm going to show Dustin how good I can two-step and fast dance."

She laughed, unable not to because her little darling was good. "I'm going to take some pictures and a video because I know just how good you are. You and your daddy used to make me smile all the time because you two could dance so well together. Yes, you were a lot shorter than him, but it didn't matter. Your daddy believed you were the best, and I agree. Oh my goodness, darlin', you made his heart sing, you were so good dancing with him."

Hazel's eyes sparkled. Oh, how wonderful they were. They were her daddy's eyes: hazel and beautiful. "Do you think he'll be smiling at me, Mama?"

"Oh sugar, your daddy is going to be cheering you on from up above. He's going to be so happy at the way you are moving forward and taking everything he taught you, and your using it to grow in heart and soul. And making it sparkle for everyone who knows he was your daddy. You shine, just like he did." Oh goodness, the tears were just spilling out and there was no stopping them.

Hazel threw her arms around her waist. "Mama, I'm so glad he was my daddy and he makes me so happy living in my heart, even though I wish he was holding my hand and dancing with me. But, Mama, he's not, and he's not doing that with you either. He might want to but he isn't. Do you think you could ever love Dustin like I do?"

Her tears flowed harder at those words. Her daughter admitted that she loved Dustin and that her daddy was happy and would be wanting her to love someone again. *But could she?* "Darlin', your daddy would be so proud of you. Just because he died, he didn't want you spending the rest of your life wishing he would come back. He's up there, cheering for you. Rooting you on. And the fact that you love a man as good as he was…"

She paused as her words filled her. *Good as he was.*

Sydney never in her entire life thought there was anyone as good as her sweet, loving Nelson. But now she knew that wasn't true. Dustin was wonderful, and he was being so amazingly good to her and her daughter. Even though they hadn't known each other that long, it felt as if they'd known each other forever. "I can't promise you anything but you know I loved your daddy with all of my heart, and he loved me the same way. But I know he's rooting for us to embrace our life and move forward. And, sweetie, you're doing that and teaching me that maybe I do need to open my heart again. So I'm going to try."

Hazel grinned at her. "Well, just like Daddy used to say, 'Girl, you just give what you've got and it'll make me happy.'"

And that was exactly what he would have said.

* * *

Dustin was determined not to let his emotions get in the way. That wedding had been eye-opening for him. And he wasn't crazy. He thought, unless she was seeing Nelson standing there in his place, that she had looked at him with love. Yes, she had yanked her gaze away when she had become aware of what she was doing, but his heart had thundered from that moment. And when he'd stopped in the aisle, her sweet darling hugged him like that, making him promise to dance with her, when he had almost planned to skip out and go home. But as if his brother had expected something was up earlier, when he'd first arrived, he'd had Dustin assure him that he would be at the reception, so he'd stay. *How had he known that he would be feeling this way?*

The two of them had always been close. Yes, they'd always read each other's minds a little bit, and something told him West had read his today.

He walked in under the large tent. The music was already playing and many couples were on the dance floor, two-stepping, as they waited for the wedding couple to be announced. He knew it would be just a few moments, so he scanned the tables and saw Sydney sitting with Millie and Jasmine Scott, who had started working at Genna's place. It was great that she'd applied and was enabling Genna and West to take a honeymoon trip out to the Grand Canyon area.

He smiled at that; she'd been with her parents all over the world but chose the canyon because she'd never been and loved looking at it. West had loved the idea, so they would be on their way soon. The McCoy Flight Charters was a private jet company they used from a group of friends over in Stonewall, a small Texas town about the size of Lone Star, surrounded by large ranches and a land full of oil. Beck McCoy was the owner of the company. Instead of buying their own jets to fly and be responsible for, they were on the top of the list and maintained their own airstrip for the flights they might need from Beck's company. And tonight was one of the most important flights ever for the newlyweds. Dustin was very happy for his brother.

And now, as he stared across the room, his gaze locked on the woman he loved. He knew he had to get on track and not, repeat *not*, mess this up.

Yes, he had promised adorable Hazel a dance and Sydney had emotionally encouraged the dance. In his heart of hearts, he knew this dealt with feelings for her husband, and then his thought was clarified by both her and Hazel that she used to dance with her daddy. He was touched deep in his heart about that. Just the thought of dancing with his own daughter one day was an enchanting vision. *But would he?* If Sydney made no changes in her life, this dream wouldn't happen for him.

CHAPTER THIRTEEN

He took a deep breath. This was not all about him. He knew that he loved that woman and that darling girl, and their loving hearts were locked to the obviously wonderful man who had loved one and helped produce the one they both loved. What kind of jerk would he be if he turned and walked away when he knew that his heart belonged to them, whether they knew it or not. Genna had told him to hang in there. And he was going to do that.

He stepped forward. His heart lurched as he wove through the tables toward Sydney. Then he saw what he hadn't been able to see earlier from where he'd been standing, what all three of the ladies were watching. At the edge of the dance floor, a potted tree hid Hazel from his view, dancing with a group of kids her age. Her adorable little dress that came down right above her ankles flowed as she twisted and spun to the music. All the kids were laughing and moving and enjoying the moment, getting into the rhythm. Even the little boys were getting it as their boots clicked and tapped on the floor to the rapid Western song.

He wanted to dance with Sydney and to dance with that sweet girl Hazel, who had blown him away when she'd asked him to come dance with her. The song ended, and he approached the table, moving in to stand beside Sydney's chair. "I see we have a dancer in the group. She's adorable and good."

Instantly, Sydney's gaze flew up to his—as he was sure the other two did, but his gaze was only focused on the woman in the chair next to him.

"She does love to dance, like I told you earlier, so whenever you want to take the challenge, jump in there and go for it."

He liked the new sound in her voice. It was as if she'd gotten control of the emotion that was clearly upsetting her earlier. It had to be hard for her; he could only imagine if that sweet little girl was his and he watched her hurting—he had seen her fighting it and that tore at him. But seeing her pain from the very beginning of losing her daddy had to tear even deeper to this dear woman who had felt it, too, and watched her child suffer. She was fighting to show a strong side and that was good.

"Well, I'll need a song as good as that one, or she might turn me down when I ask her."

"Nope." Hazel's voice had him smiling as she'd suddenly spotted him and ran over. "I'm ready to dance with you, cowboy."

He grinned and behind him, he heard her mother chuckle, which rang through him like soft, glistening crystal chimes dancing in a gentle wind. She'd chuckled. It was a relief to hear that sound of happiness when earlier he'd seen so much sadness.

He held out his hand to a smiling Hazel. "If you're up for it, I am. Now show me what you've got."

Sweet Hazel's face beamed. Her eyes, the color of walnuts with golden sizzle glistening in them, shined up at him, as if light from behind them shown through. It was amazing. "Then come on, cowboy. Let's do this."

She snagged his held-out hand and then that little toot sashayed out to the dance floor, pulling him behind her. She didn't stop at the edge of the dance floor—oh no— she swept her way out right smack in the middle, then spun toward him and grinned. She repositioned her hand in his, with their palms pressed together and her fingertips curled over the edge of his hand, between his thumb and pointer finger, as if cupping them out to their side, ready to dance.

Of course, he towered over her and had to bend slightly so his hand and hers were not beside their shoulders like a normal man and woman, but out about the level of his hips. Then she grabbed his other hand and placed it on her shoulder, like he didn't know what to do, and then she looked up at him.

"Okay, dude, lead the way," she demanded. Her sweet voice rang with authority and her eyes danced with humor and challenge.

He almost laughed out loud. "Oh, so I get to lead this dance," he said in funny disbelief.

She grinned widely, those eyes twinkling. Oh goodness, her eyes could sparkle. "Well, of course. *I'm* the female you are privileged to dance with, and you're the handsome dude. But if you can't lead, I'll take control and show you how. But I've got a feeling you can do it. Believe me, I've showed a lot of boys my age how to do this and they don't much like it. So, just so you know, I can take control."

He threw his head back and hooted with laughter. No way could he hold back. Then he looked down at her. "Well, okay, little darlin', on the beat we go." And so, they stepped into the beat of the music, and he led the way.

And that little girl didn't need leading; she could move with the smoothness of a grown pro dancer. She was great and on target; the beat never messed her up, so he added to it by pulling her hand up and releasing her shoulder and sending her on a little twirl. The kid laughed and went with it, grasping that long skirt with her free hand and holding it out so it flowed as she spun.

He was in love. This was amazing. Her hand and his stayed connected as she spun, then he guided her back, and he placed his hand on her shoulder as she let the skirt go and replaced her hand on his hip, looked up and smiled as they continued to the sound of the music.

Then she beamed up at him, and her eyes were bright with moisture. "My daddy would be so proud right now. You dance good, real good. And you know when you dance good, that helps me dance even better. That was fun. Let's keep this going."

His heart thundered and he fought back tears of sadness and tears of joy as they moved to the beat. And everyone on the dance floor paused their dancing and scooted wide and watched this little sweetheart show them how it was done.

In his heart of hearts, he sent the message: *Nelson, you knew what you were doing. And I can tell you, buddy, you are very well loved by this little girl and that sweet woman sitting at that table, watching.*

He also knew that no matter how sad he got, how down he got, these two would always have him by their side. Even if they pushed him away, he would always be on alert to be there if they needed him.

And oh how he looked forward to tomorrow.

Tomorrow, between those little goats and this little gal, there was going to be a lot of laughter, and he had a feeling she was going to be rolling on the ground, tussling with them. Heck, she might even climb up on the back of one of the donkeys and try jumping from one to the other—he might have to watch out for that. But no matter what, tomorrow was going to be more fun than the sadness that had built up all day. This wedding had been a wonderful occasion for his brother and that pretty Genna, but it also had brought a lot of sadness to these two that they had to find their way through. But tomorrow it was going to be different.

Tomorrow, they were going to make new memories that had to do with this little one, her mom, him, and a whole yard of cute little goats. His heart was ready.

* * *

Sydney had so much sadness tonight but then, watching the joy on her daughter's face as she flowed with the music, hand in hand with the man… She did her little twirls when he held her hand out there… Oh, the memories…Hazel and her daddy had loved doing all of that. And it was almost as if—and she knew it wasn't true—but it was as if Dustin was carrying her Nelson's guidance in his movements, his hands, and oh, that smile when he looked at her child. It was so heart-touching. Instead of crying now, she could do nothing but smile. She loved seeing the joy of their child, and she knew in her heart that Nelson was looking down and smiling so hugely. And there was beautiful sunshine in his hazel eyes—happiness, pride, and joy that this baby that he loved so much was having a wonderful time.

"They're beautiful out there together," Millie said as she met her eyes.

"Yes, they are. That sweet girl wanted to dance, and her daddy couldn't be here. I'm very thankful that when she asked him to dance that Dustin stepped in. And…he dances so much like Nelson did."

"I think it's adorable," Jasmine said. "It's touching. And I'm just going to say that we both saw it when he was here. Do you realize how he looks at you?"

Oh, goodness. When he'd been here moments ago, her world had stilled to only him and her, and she hadn't even thought about her tablemates watching them. "Do you see something different in his eyes when he looks at me?" She knew what they were going to say because she saw it. But was what she was seeing real, and did she want it to be?

"Oh, ho-ho." Millie chuckled deeply. "Honey, it was real. Oh, goodness."

"Oh, my goodness is right," Jasmine echoed.

Millie grinned and kept talking. "Me and my sweet guy—like you, I didn't get to be married to the love of my life very long. I never thought I'd fall in love—didn't want to. I turned off all those spouts. I've seen men looking at you; you might not have noticed, but we all see it. I used to get looked at like that when I was younger, and I turned them all away and made it clear I wasn't interested. In my heart of hearts, I didn't want anyone trying to take my Hank's place. That man could ride a bull…oh my, he was amazing. He was top of the list. Oh, he had to fight for it, but he was there. Every once in a while, he'd miss top spot in an event but his ranking hardly ever varied much. We'd go rodeo the rodeo together and we both won, me in barrel racing and him in bull riding. I ranked high in the NFR most of the time, but him—he was at the top all the time."

She smiled. "He won so many top rodeo awards and then he met that one…the one that was set to take him away from me. The one that he had ridden once before and been tossed off, and he had not liked it. But the one thing that tuff cowboy never did was throw a challenge away." Her gaze drilled into Sydney, as if directing this straight to her. "That man, he loved the challenge and he felt like one could always move him forward. And I loved him for it. But yes, challenges do sometimes have risks. And my man, *my* cowboy took that challenge and he made the ride…" she said, her voice raspy with emotion.

She paused, inhaled, then continued, "And what a ride it was. At the end of it, he landed on his feet and the rodeo clowns rushed out to get between him and the bull. He raised his arms, swept his Stetson up with one hand and stood there as everyone cheered, and he was smiling at me. But then, before anyone could tell him, the bull charged past the clowns, knocked both out of the way, put its head down, aimed his horns at my darling cowboy, trampled him horribly…and took him away from me." She sniffed.

"I witnessed it, and I see it over and over again in my head. Even after all these years. But you know that what I don't see is sadness—I see happiness, and challenge. I hear him declaring: *never give up, don't stop*. And I know the moment he was hit, the seconds before the impact, that he was happy and those words were flowing through him. And he'd warned me before we got married, that he would always step up to the challenge. Oh, he would say I love you; I love you with all of my heart, but darlin', you were a challenge."

She grinned, her face lighting up. "And to tell the truth, I was. I didn't date many men but they tried. But I was involved in my life, my goals on the back of my horses. But then he came along and just like on the back of a bull, he never quit. For two years, he was constantly being nice to me, asking me out, complimenting my looks, my smile, and my barrel racing, telling me how great I was and how much I inspired him to meet his challenges. For me, it was watching him meet his challenges; it helped me meet mine. We were a great team, if I'd give in. Finally…"

She laughed gruffly; a tear dripped from her eyes and she swiped it aside. "Finally, I rode my horse and I won. But all I could think about was him. So that night, when he came out and rode his bull, he landed on the ground like always, and I was standing right there at that fence. Those good ole clowns had gotten that bull right out of the gate. And I just climbed that fence, dropped to the ground, and strode toward him. He saw me coming, as did the fans, and he slung his hat across the arena and charged toward me, his grin so wide and happy as we met in the middle of the dirt arena. My Hank swept me into his arms and as he swept me up, we started kissing and everyone began cheering. We never stopped kissing and loving after that. We married the next day and were married for a short five years. Five wonderful years of love while fulfilling our competitive spirits together, spurring each other and celebrating together.

"But then, after that horrible night that I watched that bull charge him and trample him as if he were a simple pile of dry leaves to play in, I couldn't go back. Nothing could ever be as great and wonderful as those years with him and the things we loved. I had to find a new life, like you. A life that would help me smile again, a life that took me out of the limelight. Oh yes, that night he died made the news, and along with news of his death, those many videos taken the night we declared our love there in that arena before everyone, kissing, laughing and holding our clasped hands up as they cheered, those also made the news.

"And I came home and for a little while, I hid out on the ranch. Then I decided it was time to step out. I had watched all these people in town enjoying their business. And so I started one. So here I am, enjoying life again, a different life. But what I'm telling you, sweet girl, is you know what I felt. You do and I know it; I see it in your eyes—you feel it. But you know, you are watching that sweet little girl of yours out there and you know who is watching too, don't you?"

Sydney swiped tears away. "Yes, her daddy. And before you started talking, I was thanking him. And I was so glad that Dustin is helping her feel what she felt and loved when her daddy was alive."

Jasmine reached out and cupped her hand. "I just want to tell you both that what you two have felt is a blessing. And is not to be taken for granted. You two were so loved—not something I've ever felt, but sitting here listening to you two might help me open my heart one day. But like Millie is telling you, you shouldn't close your heart anymore because like she can, I can feel that your wonderful husband is not just up there cheering your darling daughter, but he's cheering you on too. We see your eyes. You've been trying to hide it. Deny it all you want to, but when that man is around, you come alive. So, just don't forget there could be another life of love out there for you. You can fall in love again. I believe it.

"Anyway, I needed to throw that in. I don't want to interrupt your beautiful story of love, Millie. It was so sad but beautiful, and that good man was so glad to have you rooting for him in the stands. And yes, I know you were blessed to have him rooting for you. It's hit me straight on, I've got to find strength in my own self to push my past aside and maybe look for what you've both had. I'm not ready yet but you two, with your deep, heartfelt love, even though it was short, I'm just going to tell you, you were blessed. So blessed. Anyway, who knows—if someone comes and asks me to dance, I might say yes. Might not, but at least the thought is there. I'm going to shut up now and you two can start talking again."

Millie chuckled and reached out and covered their hands with hers. "I'm not dancing with anybody, but all I want to say is you two young ladies don't have to shut your hearts, so work on getting them opened. Who knows—I never thought about it before, but sitting here with you two, I'm fifty, so maybe one day...he's going to have to be perfect, really perfect. But if that perfect man walks in, I might just accept a dance from him. So, I'm not going to totally shut the door anymore. But I'm not going to go out there and look. The day that man walks in, I hope I know. If I don't know, maybe he'll give me enough hints to help me know.

"But all I'm going to say is, Sydney, you're getting a lot of hints and everybody in this town is feeling it. We just hope you can accept it because, girl, you are up for the challenge. You are. You are one strong cookie, so don't let worry knock you down. You go for it. Anyway, maybe that's not good advice, you think, but that's just what I've got to say. And I've got to tell you that Dustin Buckley is one gorgeous challenge."

CHAPTER FOURTEEN

Dustin was waiting by the red barn for the car he knew would bring the gals he loved. The night before, he'd danced with that sweet girl until nine-thirty and she wouldn't leave the floor. She'd worked him over. He'd wanted to ask her mom to dance but in his heart of hearts he knew that was not the time. Sydney had been in a deep conversation at the table. He saw Millie and Jasmine and Sydney in a covered hand clasp toward the end and in his mind he wondered if they were praying. But he could see Millie's face—strong cowgirl Millie—and her expression was so full of sadness, then joy. She was talking and the woman didn't talk all that much.

It was well known around town that only lately had she started bonding with the town to get these dances and activities going. And everyone was rooting her on quietly. She was nice, and they all loved her. And they were proud for her and sad for her.

As he'd glanced over at them again, he couldn't look long because he'd had a little gal just leading the way. Yes, she'd told him to do that and he was, but her excitement outdid everything. Clearly, Hazel loved to dance and he knew that her daddy was watching. And Dustin was thrilled to be the man helping her and her daddy have this great night.

When Sydney finally got up from the deep and obviously touching conversation, hugged the two women she'd been sitting with, and approached them, he'd known it was time for the night to end. This sweet girl couldn't stay up till eleven or later so they'd have to call it quits at some point. But cowboys loved to dance, and obviously everybody else did too. So he knew she was coming to take her girl home. And that was good because as hard as she was dancing, if she didn't go home and get some rest, she was going to be worn out tomorrow. And he wanted her to feel good when she came out to see the goats.

"Are you ready to go home and get some rest? We have a fun day tomorrow."

She nodded to her mom and then tugged him so he knelt beside her, and she kissed him on the cheek. "Thanks. And I can't wait till tomorrow."

He'd said the same, stood, and gave Sydney a smile, then watched them leave, hand in hand. Sydney looked over her shoulder and gave him another smile, and that had sent him home. His spirits soared. He didn't know what was going to come of it, but he'd gotten two smiles from her and that made him want to dance again. But he hadn't. He'd gone home, took a shower, laid down in bed, crossed his arms on his chest and thought about Sydney and what they could have if she ever opened her heart again.

And now, standing here waiting, he saw them coming. His heart jumped, threw itself around inside him, and he felt like he had a goat romping around inside his chest with long jumps and flips. Yeah, that had to be how the goats felt—it was pure glee.

When the car pulled up, he waved for them to come over the cattle guard. He headed for their side of the car, because Hazel rode in the back seat as a child her age was supposed to do, and her gaze was locked on the goats playing across the yard. But before he could open her door, she pushed it open and bounded out of the back seat. Her mom's door opened too, and he held his hand out to her. To his startled surprise, she took it as she slipped from the seat and stood up.

"It's good to see y'all. And I can tell you that crowd of goats who are over playing on their toys are—yep, here they come. You ready?" He looked at Hazel, her bright eyes lit up.

"Oh my goodness, you bet I am. Come on! Let's go."

And off she charged, that non-scaredy-cat toward the goats and slid on her jean-covered knees, arms opened wide as the baby goats surrounded her and took her down. She was laughing and they were bleating excitedly.

Sydney pulled her hands to her chest and let out a wonderful-sounding hoot of laughter that he had not heard before. He loved it.

"Oh my goodness, they're not going to hurt her, are

they? I'm kind of figuring they're not but look—she loves it."

"They aren't going to hurt her. They will think she's their best friend. She's romping with them like she's one of them."

"Oh, look she's rolling and they are too." Sydney's eyes were glued to her child.

"The little kids are having a frolicking good time. Come on, let's go meet them. You don't have to get on the ground and roll around with them, I promise. They'll just prop their front feet on your knees and let out a cute maaing call up to you. It's their way of saying, *Please pet us. Please pet us. Please, please pet us.*"

She laughed, looking him straight in the eyes. "*You* are funny."

He grinned. "Sometimes, but I don't know—it might be by accident."

"Maybe," she said. "But I don't think so."

Once again, his heart went wild, far wilder than he'd ever imagined it could go with the need to lean forward and kiss Sydney's smiling lips. He mentally bopped himself in the forehead. *Get a grip, dude.*

He needed a diversion, so he led the way to the goats that instantly were distracted from the active girl running and romping with as many that wanted to tag along with her. He tapped his legs, and those that weren't romping with Hazel came to them; they immediately lifted up and placed hooves on his and Sydney's knees.

"Hey there, fellas." He reached down and petted their heads.

Smiling and cooing, Sydney did the same to a musical of maas and naas. "I love these. And look at Hazel. Okay, so just seeing her running and playing—I'm getting some of these. I'll have a special, good-sized area built over to the side of the house with plenty of views from the room on the side where the kitchen windows are and the view from the side windows of the living room. It would mean if she were playing with them, I would be able to watch her from time to time while I was cooking."

He smiled widely. "You know she's going to love that." He couldn't take his eyes off her. And, to his surprise, she didn't shift her eyes away. "You are a wonderful mother."

"Thank you. I worried so much after I lost Nelson that I wouldn't be good enough. He was a wonderful father, and I feared so badly that I'd fail and never live up to his wonderful ways." She smiled and watched her baby. Then she looked back at him. "She takes after her father and like he did, that sweet girl tries so hard to protect me. And now, she's working hard to get me to stretch myself."

He saw it clearly and before he could stop himself, he reached up and placed his palm along her soft cheek and was startled when she leaned her face into it. Her beautiful emerald eyes brightened as she held his gaze.

"I'm drawn to you, Dustin. I tried all last night at the dance to deny it but finally, after I got home, away from watching you be so wonderful to my child, I knew that I...I had fallen in love with you."

His heart dropped to his feet. He swallowed hard; his throat had gone dry and his breath had taken a trip to the moon. *She loved him.*

"My mama told you she loves you. And you are just staring at her."

The declaration of sweet Hazel drew his frozen gaze from the glistening eyes of her mother.

Hazel popped her hands to her hips and grinned. "We love you, Dustin. And I think you love us."

His heart rose on helium back to where it belonged, and his lungs filled as he sucked in air. A huge smile busted across his face as he looked from the adorable, unbelievable little girl to her wonderful mother. The woman he loved. He blinked tears and smiled. "I'm having trouble speaking but…" He opened his arms and to his joy, both Sydney and Hazel flew into them. And all around them, the goats let out the joyful maa-maa sounds of happy goats.

"I do love you," he said against Sydney's ear.

She turned her head, and her lips were next to his. "I love you so very much, and I feel so very blessed to have found two men like you and Nelson. But Dustin, I love you for the man that you are and the undeniable way that you felt for us, but didn't try to destroy how we felt for Nelson. You are you, and *that's* the main reason I had to admit to myself that I love you. I wanted you as mine. And now I'm asking you if you would have me—

"

"Yes," he said. "Wait, you were asking me to marry you, right?"

"Mama," Hazel's voice trembled, "is he going to be my daddy? I mean, my daddy in heaven is mine forever, but I want to dance with Dustin whenever I want and maybe we can snuggle on the couch and watch one of them shows you like together."

"Darlin', I think he just said yes. Am I right? Are we about to become a family?"

His heart thundered. "Yes. We're getting married and building a goat yard to play in and always remember this moment we shared with them." And then, he reached down and lifted Hazel with his arm, and she wrapped her arms around his neck and her mama's.

"So, is the wedding tomorrow?"

He chuckled and looked at his beautiful, wonderful, loving, soon-to-be wife. "Might not be able to get a license by tomorrow but how about Wednesday? Or, if you want, we can do it any time you two decide."

"Wednesday," they said together.

He was in heaven. "Wednesday it is."

EPILOGUE

Dustin held the pole in place for the new goat pen as his cousin Ace, the youngest of the family, poured the concrete mixture into the hole.

Ace looked up at him from his kneeling position as he poured the concrete. He grinned. "It's hard to believe that you live at this bed-and-breakfast now. This place is going to be full this weekend. Is that taking some getting used to?"

"It might, but I'm good with it not being the ranch. I love the ranch, but I love those two beauties more and I'm glad to be here."

"That's great. I'm glad for you, and when we get all these goats playing in this pen, looking for affection, y'all guests coming this weekend are going to be entertained." He finished getting the concrete in the hole. "And Grandma would have loved knowing that we weren't just carrying on her love of goats at the ranch but spreading it out for all these people to enjoy. All these people who come to this beautiful B&B are going to probably come back just to play."

Dustin grinned as Ace rose. This was the last pole to cement and then they'd start the wiring that would keep the goats inside instead of letting them roam free. "I've been here two great weeks since we had our quick family wedding, and I have to say that I love the ranch and drive out there for work, but I love living here with my girls. Yep, there's going to be a lot of people at the place, on the weekends especially, but I'm loving it. This weekend is the dance. We're excited about this big house being full. Every room is booked with more than one person, and they're so looking forward to time here and in town. And this time, it's all from Jasmine's mom and her friends.

"I tell you, Hazel and her mom are excited about getting the goats in time for all the guests to see and hopefully enjoy. When everyone gets here on Friday, they'll get to see them. Sydney is cooking up a storm getting ready and everything is wonderful. While we bring in goats, she'll be making that house smell delicious. She can cook. I married her because I loved her *and* her wonderful skills in the kitchen. And look over there—she and Millie are brightening this yard up with wonderful flowers. That Millie is a great person, and I think she helped Sydney open her heart. I'll always owe her."

Ace looked over where they were working and smiled. "They look like they are having fun. But you know good and well you told Hazel to go work with the ladies because we were pouring the concrete and that cutie pie would rather be over here helping us with these goat pens."

Dustin grinned. "Well, we're finishing the concrete, then we're going to call her over here so she can help us put up the fence wire. I know she wants to help but I didn't want her to be here while we were working on the concrete. Plus, they enjoy her helping them. That sweet Millie kind of took to them and has been helping them redo all those flower beds. She needed sweet Hazel over there helping her. Millie's been here helping them every day this week after she closes her store. She's been coming here and planting in all these beautiful flower beds. The guests are going to love them and will probably come out and sit in some of these sitting areas Sydney set up. Even if they didn't have the cute little goats we're going to put in this play area, they'd have a great place for the visitors to enjoy conversations and sunsets."

"Sounds great. And it's good to see you so happy, man."

"I am extremely happy. And the goats are going to make it even better, make Hazel even happier. Hazel is going to pick out her favorites. I think we're going to start out with four and then we can grow them as much as she wants. Let them have babies, even, to grow the kids. And speaking of kids, Hazel already asked me when me and her mom are going to give her a baby sister or brother."

His cousin's grin widened. "You going to get ahead of West and Genna and make Aunt Christine happy?"

Dustin grinned widely, remembering how his heart had jumped at the question and then seeing his amazing wife's obvious delight at her daughter's bright-eyed inquiry. He'd told her that he and her mama would talk about it and let her know. He smiled. Babies were something he'd shut his mind down on years earlier and now wanted more than anything besides Sydney's and Hazel's love. They were going to increase their family soon. And if they decided to grow it larger, they would build a house here within eyesight of the B&B, on land that was hers and his, land that had been ranched for years by her grandpa and now him and his brothers and cousins. "I think we might try to give them a run for their money. Of course, you know how Mom is already embracing Hazel as her granddaughter, so technically we're already ahead."

Ace pushed him on the arm. "Yep, that little girl is dearly loved. And my friend, my cousin, my buddy who didn't really date all that much after you came back from college with your heart broken—then boom, Sydney moved to town and you were gone. Anyway, we're all really happy. I don't know, man. Maybe you and West are walking with high steps now and look really happy. I don't know if I'm ready to get married yet. I am the youngest, even if only by a few seconds or minutes, so I may have to think about it a bit."

Dustin saw the hint of true curiosity in his cousin's eyes. Ace was twenty-six and the youngest, if only by a little bit since his twin brother, Hunter beat him out by a few minutes. In their entire family the twins were the youngest, so Dustin hadn't felt like they'd be next in line to fall in love. But who knew who it would be—finding the magic of love was an extraordinary wonder and he was so thrilled that he'd been the second in line of his family to experience his destiny.

"Hey, can I come work now?" Hazel called from where she knelt beside Millie. Millie grinned as she looked at them, and so did Sydney.

"Come on. I don't have to hold this straight anymore—it's hardened enough to leave it alone for a bit. Let's go talk to my girls. That way she won't be coming over here and stepping in the concrete."

"You know, you could have her put her handprints in that right there like we used to do sometimes."

He smiled. "Good idea. Little cousin, I think you're going to make a great dad one day."

"Hey, don't start getting any ideas. I'm going to be satisfied being hopefully a great uncle for now."

"Okay, sounds good. Hazel, want to come make a handprint in this concrete?"

She jumped to her feet. "Yay! Come on, Mama and Millie. Come watch."

Grinning, they all got to their feet and came over.

"Okay," he said when Hazel reached him. "It's good you've got your short-sleeve T-shirt on because we'll do this and then wash your hands and you'll be all good."

"If I'd had a long-sleeve shirt on and I made a mess, I'd throw it in the trash cuz this is worth losing a shirt. Right, Mama?"

Sydney chuckled. "Right. This will be a great idea to have your little handprints here, marking the positive change in our life."

Her gaze rested on his, and he felt her love all the way to his toes.

"So very true. But thank good ole Uncle Ace here for the great idea."

Hazel grinned up at her uncle. "Thanks. I like this

a lot."

"I do too." Ace grinned.

"Now, bend down and spread your fingers out a little bit," Dustin said, already knelt down and waiting as Hazel dropped to her knees and spread her small fingers wide. He was glad that they'd dug the hole wide enough to support the metal pole and to take her small imprints too. "Now, keep your thumbs almost touching and your fingers like that, and lean forward and push them down into the cement just enough you'll leave their form in the soft cement."

She grinned in delight. "This is gonna be fun." And then she leaned forward and pressed those hands in.

He was ready to grab her wrist if she pressed too hard, but the cement had hardened just enough that she did it perfectly.

"Great. Now straight up when you pull your hands out. Go ahead and bring them out."

She did that perfectly, too, then looked at the little bit of cement around her fingers. "Now what?"

He grinned at her as Ace handed him the water hose they'd used to mix the cement. He took it and held it over her hands as Ace reached down and turned the knob of the faucet the two of them had run out here the day before to make getting water to the pens easy. He let the water run over her hands as she automatically began to rub them together.

"This is fun. How's that?" She held them up, and he inspected them.

"Looks good to me."

Instantly, she wiped her clean, wet hands dry on the front of her shirt and looked over at her handprints. "Mama, do you like that?"

"I love it."

"I do too," Millie added. "I have some at the base of the steps of the house I live in that my dad built when I was your age. It's hard to look at them and believe I was ever that little."

Hazel grinned up at the older, tall but lanky lady. "You might not be little like me, but you have purdy hands."

"Well, thank you." Millie held her long-fingered, slender hands up and smiled. The gold wedding band on her left ring finger glistened in the sunlight.

Dustin looked at it, and his heart gripped. His wonderful wife had lost her first husband after only six years; so had this beautiful older woman, and she still wore her wedding ring. He'd actually asked Sydney one evening while holding her left hand out here under the moonlight why she'd taken off her wedding ring after losing Nelson because he'd noticed that Millie still wore hers all these years later. Sydney had looked him in the eyes. "I made myself do it the year after he'd died. I put it in my jewelry box to keep it safe for Hazel to wear as a ring one day. But I never thought I'd taken it off to get myself open for falling in love again and a new ring on my left ring finger. Now, I have your ring and Nelson's to pass to his daughter to wear on her right finger if she wants to or to use as her wedding ring. I've been so very blessed to have two true loves."

Her words had meant so much to him, and he knew Nelson didn't mind. He could feel in his heart that her first husband—like him, her second husband—felt blessed to have called her his, even for a short time. Dustin hoped and prayed he got to call her his wife for a long, happy life. But he was blessed and knew it.

Now, as he looked at Millie's ring and then her face and the way her gaze had lingered on that ring, he suddenly wondered whether there was going to be another love in her life one day. She was a wonderful woman and he really held a warm place in his heart for her because it had been her and her words of love to Sydney that had helped Sydney see her love for him. He would always owe Millie for her help in his happiness. Maybe there would one day be another man for her. One who would love her as deeply as he loved Sydney.

In that moment, she let her hands down, and her gaze met his.

"You do have pretty hands, Millie, and a pretty heart." Sydney leaned into him as he lifted his arm out in invitation. He looked at her, then at Millie. "We will forever be grateful for you."

Millie smiled. "I'm so glad to see your smiling faces, and I know you three," she looked down at a smiling Hazel, "are going to touch the lives of a lot of people here at this beautiful B&B. So, just so you know, I'm always available to help in any way. Flower beds, or working if you need me on the weekends while y'all take a fun weekend off somewhere. I'd enjoy hosting some of your guests for you."

He hitched a brow. "Now that might be something we take you up on. But first, me and my brothers have to get back out there on the ravine and make sure that mountain lion has taken off. I think everyone is safe while I'm here but we have to go out and look for any signs of that lion at least one more time. Because I have to make sure everyone is safe and I have to walk over the fallen tree with Hazel."

"Yes, we do have to do that," Hazel squealed.

"We'll do it after I take another look out there and we get this first weekend of guests in and out happy here at the house."

He looked back at Millie's puzzled expression as she looked at Sydney and hitched a brow. *What was going on?*

"Oh," Sydney gasped. "I got so involved in marrying you that I forgot." She grinned. "I've been needing to tell you that you need to have a long conversation with *Millie*. This amazing woman and I talked about the lions, and I got so busy that I never mentioned it. This lady knows a *lot* about mountain lions. And I have to tell you that I don't think they're around anymore."

He looked at Millie in surprise. She was a horsewoman. "So Millie, what do you know that I obviously need to know?"

Millie grinned. "You may already know everything I do since you did research but well, your sweetness there was telling me how worried you were about even the possibility one is out there. But I have to tell you that my daddy and my granddaddy were hunters and knew a lot about lions. But I'm the one who is obsessed with things and dug deeper and they always asked me any questions they had. So basically, I'm a bit of a nerd when it comes to getting curious about something and digging deep. And it lodges in my brain and stays. So, I can tell you that you're going to be like Sydney there and you're going to know that that mountain lion— single, as in one—they don't travel together, and they are very dominant of their land, so rarely are there two of them unless it's mating time or you have a mama and cubs. But, still they travel on their land, which is a lot, like around a hundred square miles. As I'm sure you know, there are six hundred and forty acres to a square mile. Those cats like to roam and I'm pretty sure it will be a while before they come back around. But you haven't found any more dead cows, right?"

"Um, no, and the cows have been back there the last two weeks. We decided to take a chance, and truthfully, I'd like a cow as a distraction from Hazel and Sydney. So I wanted to set them loose back there and see what happened. I hate to say that, but I love these gals too much to risk them."

Sydney wrapped her arms around his waist and smiled up at him. "We know you're not just being mean. But I have to say, after hearing all that Millie—smart Millie—had to say freed me from fear. She is amazing. And lions are interesting. I have a feeling she's probably full of amazing information on a lot of things. She's like a walking, talking encyclopedia that digs deep. But I think that me and Hazel and all your animals are safe. That lion has probably moved on."

He grinned down at his beautiful, adorable, and spun-his-heart-out-of-control wife. "Well, okay, darling. Me and Miss Millie will have a long conversation and if what you're saying and her knowledge is as much on point as you say and she convinces me, then I'll relax a little. But I just have to tell you that you signed on with me, and I'm here by your side to look out for you and this *amazing* little girl." He wrapped his arm around Hazel as she came to stand beside him and grinned up at him. "So even if it's not lions that I'll be watching out for, I'm going to be watching out for anything and everything that might hurt y'all. And I'm going to run it off. And I have a feeling I'm going to get help from your daddy in heaven." He smiled at Hazel.

The delightful girl hugged him around the waist and laughed. "I know, I know. Daddy knew what he was doing when he helped you find us. And maybe he put that lion out there so we could meet you."

Ace busted out laughing and so did Millie. It was all so touching and yes, funny, to look through this loveable girl's eyes at what was going on around her.

"Well, little woman," Ace drawled. "You could be right, because we've never seen a lion out there before and to find a lion or at least the leftovers he left behind, it kind of put Dustin on edge a little. But when he rescued your mom from that water and you two entered his life, I don't think there's been anything sad in his world since. The man walks around like he's walking on clouds and with that cute little face of yours, I can see why."

Millie grinned at him, and Hazel walked over and looked up at her uncle. "Uncle Ace, maybe you need to find you a woman who will make you smile like that. You're cute, you know."

Ace laughed, and Dustin almost busted out laughing at his cousin, who loved horses and fishing. He didn't feel as though his cousin would ever find anyone to slip into the space between those two itineraries that took up most of his days and thoughts.

Then Dustin looked at Sydney, his beautiful wife, who was smiling up at him. "Well, I was about to say that I doubt Ace will ever fall in love, but I don't know, the way I see it, when the right woman enters his life," he smiled down at Sydney. "Then love is going to happen."

He looked at Ace, who stared at him as if he were crazy. Millie was grinning widely, and again he wondered whether she would ever have the wonder of falling in love again. And then he looked down at Hazel, who was smiling so happily.

"Yep, when it happens, it happens, and there is no stopping it. *And* you're not going to want it to stop, cowboy."

They all looked at Ace now, and Ace looked a bit bewildered, then grinned. "Well, the day it's supposed to happen, it'll happen. But I have a feeling it's not going to be too soon. Matter of fact, Hazel, have you been fishing?"

"No, I haven't in a long, long time but I think it's going to be fun."

"Yes, it is. You going to go with me?"

She put her hands on her hips and looked up at him. "You know I am. I'm in for any adventure you fellas who are now my uncles can take me on. I love life here. It is wonderful, and I am not going to stay at home all the time. I'm going to become a cowgirl. I'm going to rope horses. I'm going to herd cows, play with and raise goats, *and* I'm going to fish like you love to do."

They all laughed.

Dustin and Sydney touched each other's cheek, and he gave her a quick peck on the lips. Oh, how he loved her and the life she'd opened up to him.

"Okay then—sounds like a perfect plan, Hazel," he said. "Now, who is ready to go build some goat pens?"

More Books by Hope Moore

Billionaire Cowboys of Lone Star, Texas

Forever Love'n Cowboy

Sweet Love'n Cowboy

Heart Love'n Cowboy

Love Catch'n Cowboy

McCoy Billionaire Brothers

Her Billionaire Cowboy's Fake Marriage

Her Billionaire Cowboy's Fake Wedding Fiasco

Her Billionaire Cowboy's Trouble in Paradise

Her Billionaire Cowboy's Secret Baby Surprise

Her Billionaire Cowboy's Second Chance Romance

Her Billionaire Cowboy Fake Fiancé

Her Billionaire Cowboy's Inconvenient Marriage Blessing

Billionaire Cowboys of True Love, Texas

Billionaire Cowboy's Runaway Bride

Billionaire Cowboy's Wedding Crasher

Her Billionaire Cowboy's Hill Country Proposal

Billionaire Cowboy Auctioned at Christmas

Billionaire Cowboy's Dream Come True

About the Author

Hope Moore is the pen name of an award-winning author who lives deep in the heart of Texas surrounded by Christian cowboys who give her inspiration for all of her inspirational sweet romances. She loves writing clean & wholesome, swoon worthy romances for all of her fans to enjoy and share with everyone. Her heartwarming, feel good romances are full of humor and heart, and gorgeous cowboys and heroes to love. And the spunky women they fall in love with and live happily-ever-after.

When she isn't writing, she's trying very hard not to cook, since she could live on peanut butter sandwiches, shredded wheat, coffee...and cheesecake why should she cook? She loves writing though and creating new stories is her passion. Though she does love shoes, she's admitted she has an addiction and tries really hard to stay out of shoe stores. She, however, is not addicted to social media and chooses to write instead of surf FB - but she LOVES her readers so she's working on a free novella just for you and if you sign up for her newsletter she will send it to you as soon as its ready! You'll also receive snippets of her adventures, along with special deals, sneak peaks of soon-to-be released books and of course any sales she might be having.

She promises she will not spam you, she hates to be spammed also, so she wouldn't dare do that to people she's crazy about (that means YOU). You can unsubscribe at any time.

Sign up for my newsletter at:
www.subscribepage.com/hopemooresignup

I can't wait to hear from you.

Hope Moore~
Always hoping for more love, laughter and reading for you every day of your life!